Fate at the Wi.
The Pink Shell S

Volume 1

Kaya Quinsey Holt

coco rose books

Dedication

This one's for you, dad.

Copyright Page

Fate at the Wisteria Estate: The Pink Shell Shores Series Volume 1

A Coco Rose Books Publication

Copyright © Kaya Quinsey Holt

All rights reserved.

Title page adapted from iStockphoto.com images

First e-book edition February 2020

Fate at the Wisteria Estate: The Pink Shell Shores Series Volume 1 is a work of fiction. Names, characters, places, and events are the products of the author's imagination and are used fictitiously. Any resemblance to actual events, locales, or persons, living or dead, is entirely coincidental.

www.kayaquinsey.com

Chapter One

The New Year always brings out the best intentions in people, at least, according to Aribella "Bell" Lacroix. That's why she had moved in to her new home in Pink Shell Shores two days before the old year expired. She had celebrated the New Year's Eve countdown to midnight surrounded by boxes piled higher than her shoulders, at varying stages of unpacking. At 14 Oyster Lane, Bell's new seaside cottage was coming along. Within the few days she had been there, she had unpacked thirty-six boxes. There had been three rounds of tears, a bottle of cabernet sauvignon, and endless calls to Lacey Lacroix–her identical twin-sister. Now Bell was almost completely unpacked. And it was a few minutes after noon on New Year's Day.

"What do you think, Georgia?"

The ancient one-eyed English toy spaniel glanced up at her from her plush bed and sniffed at nothing in particular. Bell had rescued her from the animal shelter a few years earlier. Georgia showed her approval by responding with a nonchalant exercise of licking herself.

Bell smiled and looked around the living room. "It's perfect."

The putty colored walls of the two-bedroom, three-bathroom bungalow already had photos of her and Lacey from their childhood, pictures of her parents in their post-retirement Florida house, and the medley of artwork she had collected from her travels in the Mediterranean all of those summers ago...

As if on cue, her iPhone rang.

"I'm done!" Bell pronounced the second she had pressed reply.

In the background was the familiar sound of her twin nieces, Presley and Olivia. They were fighting over something, which made for loud and distracting noises.

"Like, *everything*? You must be exhausted! Didn't you sleep?" Lacey asked, louder than usual to be heard over the commotion. Lacey didn't sound convinced. Bell couldn't blame her. It had taken Bell over a year to settle into her last apartment outside of Boston. A few weeks earlier, while she had been packing to move to Pink Shell Shores, Bell had even found a couple of still-packed boxes in the back of a closet. She couldn't bring herself to tell Lacey about them.

"No, I'm fine. This is so exciting, how could I sleep? I know you don't believe me. But that's why you, Gunner, and the girls have to come visit me in a few weeks. Seriously, Lace–I have a guest room for you and Gunner, and the girls won't mind a blow up mattress. It's–it's a different world down here."

Bell looked around her new home with wide and reddish eyes, still hardly believing that this was now her reality. A shiver of excitement ran down her spine. She thought back to the first moment she laid eyes on Pink Shell Shores only a few days before. A few weeks earlier, Bell had accepted a new job. A prestigious job. Just thinking about it created butterflies.

She had accepted and signed a contract as a wedding and venue coordinator at an amazing vacation destination, known as The Wisteria Estate. It was a renowned venue for weddings and a high-end boutique hotel. Located smack dab in the middle of Pink Shell Shores in North Carolina, it had everything: glamor, nature, scenery, romance. She had been so excited; she accepted immediately without so much as having been near the small coastal town. She had been ready for a change. Scratch that—she was *desperate*.

Within the past month, Nigel McLeary (her ex-boyfriend of *many* years) had gotten married. Thinking about it made her stomach churn. As if that wasn't bad enough, it was to a girl he had known for only six months. It didn't help matters much that Nigel was also the manager of The Saint Thomas Hotel. It was also where Bell had worked as a wedding and venue coordinator for the last five years. To make matters even worse, The Saint Tom (as staff called it) was flooded with memories. Where Nigel had first asked her out. Their first kiss. That room where they had first... Plus, so many reminders of the buddy-buddy persona that Nigel had tried to cultivate with her since their breakup that seemed phony on the best days. It was patronizing at the worst. It got to be too much.

As if the universe was trying to give her more of a giant nudge to get away from Saint Thomas and Saint Nigel, her apartment complex developed a major foundational crack because of a sinkhole. It caused the city to condemn the entire building. Later, the residents of the apartment were told it would be six months before they were allowed to move back in. There were major structural repairs that needed to be taken care of. Bell had barely enough time between applying to the job at the Wisteria Estate, getting accepted, and packing up her boxes to say goodbye to Lacey, Gunner, and the girls.

Now, as she paced in the living room of her cozy house in Pink Shell Shores, it felt like ages ago that she filled the trunk space under the hood of her mint-green Volkswagen Super-beetle with the last six moving boxes she didn't trust to give to "Cheapo Movers is Us!". She was off and running for the eleven-hour road trip from Boston to Pink Shell Shores. The Superbeetle had been a hand-me-down from her father, he on-ly drove it during the summer, and now that it was considered a vintage machine it was increasing in value every year.

Bell had a thing for vintage vehicles, cars, trucks—anything with a motor built before 1980. If she hadn't been a wedding planner, she would work in a museum of modern transporta-tion. She would miss the crew at Mechanical Joe's who kept her machine in tip-top shape. Sitting behind the wheel, shifting up and down hills, she felt nothing but confidence.

The VW carried her with Georgia in the passenger seat along the agricultural land and highways had eventually given way to Carolinian forests, pastel-colored shingled houses, and old colonial manors. As Bell drove into her new town, Pink Shell Shores had made her think if Nantucket and Charleston had a baby town, and then shrunk it...

Lacey's voice snapped Bell back to the present moment. "Bell? Bell? You still there?"

"Oh yeah, just lost in thought. Sorry. What's up?"

"You know we'd all love to come down and visit, Bell, but the girls just started first grade and we don't want to disrupt their routine or anything."

"Oh well, sure, that makes sense. Wow! Grade one."

It still surprised her whenever she heard how old the twins–the *new* set of twins–were getting. Lacey having twins was exciting given that everyone loves a twin-who-is-having-twins story. But the real surprise to Bell and their parents had been that Lacey was only 21-years-old when she and Gunner got pregnant. To everyone's amazement, Gunner had cleaned up his party-boy ways right away. He had proposed, and they had a small wedding ceremony for their respective immediate families. Thinking about back when Gunner used to pound back tequilas four nights a week made Bell stifle a giggle. He used to be a known regular to the bouncers at the best clubs in Boston. Now, Bell couldn't think of a more responsible man. He was a partner at an insurance brokerage. He and Lacey were members at an exclusive member-only tennis club. He drank red wine only on special occasions and spoiled his kids at Christmas.

"Plus, Gunner's been busy at work," Lacey added with a touch of pride.

"Amazing!" she said with a little too much punctuation.

Bell always forced a little excitement into her tone whenever her sister talked about Gunner. There was one quirk of his that drove her nuts. He had this way of remembering *everything*. Especially embarrassing facts she had said in a moment of letting her guard down. And he often brought them up at unsavory moments. Not maliciously, but in a way that made Bell wonder if his parents had skipped the lesson on tact.

You've gotten into an accident before and were deemed at fault, right Bell?

You cry every time you hear The Cranberries, right Bell?

You used to read wedding magazines and pretend you were getting married, right Bell?

You've been a bridesmaid—what is it?—four times now, right Bell?

You haven't had any other serious relationships other than Nigel, right Bell?

Changing the subject, Bell brought up the one topic she knew Lacey was sure to bring up anyway. She took a deep breath, psyching herself up.

"Well, speaking of significant others, the dating pool in Pink Shell Shores sure looks slim."

Bell had already looked through at the dating app on her phone, swiping through the photos and description of potential matches in the area. One of them had a fantastic picture of himself at the beach, but that was before she read on his bio that he was also into 'nun chucks'. Another who seemed very transparent that he wasn't looking for something serious, *One man, looking for love on the half shell.* She shuddered thinking about the only other potential match–a man who had a long list of deal breakers including 'women who cry during movies'. What was wrong with that?

Anyway, Bell had moved to Pink Shell Shores for her career. *Not* to fall in love.

"Just make sure you don't settle," Lacey said wisely but routinely. Bell had been hearing this same line from her since the breakup. Sometimes, she finished the adage with the word 'again'.

"You know, you could have told me you never liked Nigel. At least, near the end."

"*Pfft*. Like you would have listened. Promise me you won't go for someone who takes you for granted?"

"Lace–it's not like I intentionally set out to meet guys like that. It just happened. One time."

"For five years!" Lacey almost screeched. The play-fighting sounds in the background got louder, before Bell heard a loud crash.

"Lacey? Everything okay?"

"Presley! Olivia! What did I tell you about touching the china? Sorry Bell, gotta run. I'll call you tomorrow."

"Bye Lace. Love you unches and funches and bunches!" It was how they had said goodbye to each other in those few years when they were put in different classrooms all those years ago. Somehow, over the last few years, it had gotten picked up again.

"Unches and funches and bunches!" Lacey said distractedly, before hanging up.

Bell could hear the roar of the Atlantic outside her backyard. Somehow, in a competitive rental market, she had snagged an oceanfront cottage. To boot, it was only a short walk from the downtown. As the realtor had mentioned over the phone, few people were looking for entire houses in Pink Shell Shores in the winter months. The house was typically rented out to families in the spring and summer as a vacation property. But the owner of the house was more than happy to have someone look after the place year-round.

Georgia looked up from her bed on the floor, near the unlit fireplace, and looked towards the door longingly with her one-eye. Now that the house was settled and unpacked, Bell could do what she had promised herself she would: explore Pink Shell Shores.

"Alright, Georgia. Let's go for a walk. C'mon girl, you can do it."

As Bell walked towards the door to grab the harness from the cubby, the senior canine stretched herself to her feet and made her way to the door. Georgia was slowly wagging her tail, her mouth lolling open in anticipation. Bell fastened the light gray leather leash to Georgia's quartz studded leather harness. If there was any other dog more spoiled than Georgia, Bell would be surprised. Georgia had had a hard life before Bell had adopted her. Now, Bell wanted to give Georgia the best that life could offer. She grabbed her own faux-shearling coat, which she had owned for the last seven years, pulling it over her pink knit sweater.

"Okay Georgia. Let's go explore our new home," as they both stepped out into the open air.

Georgia snuffed at their faded lawn and trembled in de-lighted excitement. She dropped to the ground and wriggled on her back, delighting in scratching her modest winter coat from her hide. It was significantly warmer than where they had just come from and Bell also unzipped her jacket. Bell couldn't look straight. She kept getting distracted, her eyes darting to the other houses on Oyster Lane. Her new home—a small white-shingled bungalow with two simple Doric columns framing the peach-colored door—sat across from a grand colonial mansion, complete with two-story Corinthian columns. Oyster Lane was a unique mix of these old colonial estate-like homes and small pastel-colored shingled cottages.

They made their way to the downtown through the windy streets, marveling all the while at the small touches that the town seemed keen on. Oyster shells were embedded into the street signs. Oversized wreaths hung from the wrought-iron lamp posts. The salty air made Bell feel wide-awake. Her eyes widened as they turned onto Pink Shell Drive, the main street in the little town. Pastel pink, purple, blue, and green stucco townhouses lined the street. Swirling wrought iron balconies were perched on the second story of the four-story buildings. Old-fashioned signs hung above the doors of the main floor shops. Neatly trimmed hedges and boxwoods adorned the outer edges of the sidewalks.

"Georgia, I don't think we're in Boston anymore," she whispered to the small dog who trotted by her side. Georgia looked up with complete understanding and wondered whether it meant that it would be a good time to pee.

Families and friends wandered down Pink Shell Drive, popping in and out of mom-and-pop shops and family-run restaurants. Everyone walked at a leisurely pace. It was Sunday and New Year's Day after all. Still, it was a startling contrast to the city streets she was accustomed to. Even Georgia seemed surprised, as the dog drew nearer to Bell, and whining enough to make Bell pick her up. As they passed by a building, painted in shocking pink, the inviting scent of freshly baked shortbread and hot coffee wafted out. The door jingled as a friendly looking couple emerged. Bell looked through the window where a small sign saying *Pets Welcome, Children Must Be On A Leash* had been displayed. A sign hung above the door and was shaped as a pink teapot with the name *Tea Readings* written in gold font. It made sense as soon as she walked into the cafe. Walls upon walls and small nooks of books were stacked along every available space of the narrow coffee, tea, and bake shop. The unmistakable old book smell mingled with that of freshly baked goods. There was a quiet chatter from families sipping hot chocolate and weary-looking parents drinking coffee. Over hidden speakers, a New Orleans-style brass band played quietly.

Bell made her way to the brass-clad countertop, Georgia still in her arms.

"Well, isn't he a cutie. Or is she a she?" said the woman from behind the counter. The woman wore a stylish silk head-wrap, her hair tousled through the opening on top. She spoke with a New Orleans accent. Bell could only detect that because it was where her mother was born.

Bell smiled and stroked Georgia's fuzzy head. "She's a *she*. Her name is Georgia."

"I should have known. Look at that harness. She's a little princess, isn't she?"

The woman reached out and stroked Georgia's head, as Georgia made happy chirping noises. Bell immediately warmed to her. It wasn't often that people commented on Georgia's appearance *in a good way* right off the bat, like so often happened with other dogs. More typically, people asked what had happened to Georgia's missing eye (Bell didn't know, since Georgia was a rescue) or why Georgia was so shy and skittish around new people (she had rescued her from a puppy mill). But Bell thought Georgia was the cutest thing on earth.

"Are you from New Orleans?" Bell ventured as the woman washed her hands in the nearby sink. Almost as soon as the words were out, Bell noticed a painting on the only section of the wall that wasn't covered in books–a fleur-de-lis made of crushed shells. Bingo.

"Born and raised," the woman said, hand outstretched, as she shook Bell's hand comfortably. "Moved here to be with my wife, Penny. I'm Chantal."

"It's nice to meet you. I'm Aribella, but everyone calls me Bell. My family is from New Orleans too."

Chantal's brow furrowed. "But you're not. I can tell from your accent. Are you from... Boston?"

Bell smiled. "We grew up in a small town in Louisiana before my dad got a job in Boston. I lived there from when I was ten."

"Now what on earth brings you and Georgia all the way from Boston to Pink Shell Shores?"

Bell blushed. "I'm the new venue coordinator at the Wisteria Estate. I start tomorrow, actually."

Chantal let out a low whistle and called to the back. "Hey, Penny? Come on out here a sec." Within moments, a startlingly beautiful middle-aged woman with multiple necklaces and blue tipped shoulder length hair emerged from behind the curtain. "We've got a new local to Pink Shell Shores. This is Bell and her little dog Georgia."

Penny's face lit up. "Welcome. I will have to do your reading then at some point." Bell's expression must have given away her confusion. "Yes, it's me. I'm the clairvoyant, from the name?" Penny laughed. "Well, we thought it was very clever. The Tea Reading." Penny shook her head admiringly. "Actually, I thought it was brilliant. Chantal came up with it. Anyway, you let me know when you're ready."

Bell had never had her fortune told before, but she was intrigued. Georgia let out a whine from beneath her arm. "I should get going for today," she said, motioning with her free hand towards a wriggling Georgia, who still had not yet found the ideal place to pee and wondered when they would be back outside where the opportunity would surely abound. "But another time for sure."

"What are you having today?" Chantal asked.

"London fog, please and thanks." Bell got out her wallet before Chantal shooed it away. "Please. First one is on the house. And happy New Year! You're part of the community now. Welcome to Pink Shell Shores."

Chapter Two

The Wisteria Estate was even larger and grander in person than Bell had imagined. As majestic as they were, the professionally taken photographs Bell had gawked at on the website didn't seem to do it justice. The white stucco Italianate manor, once the home of the original settlers of Pink Shell Shores in 1860, was surrounded by elegant and well-maintained gardens and hedges. There was a limestone patio with light pink painted wrought iron patio sets. Of course, there was wisteria *everywhere*.

There was wisteria clinging to and climbing up the Wisteria Estate itself. Wisteria swirled around tree branches and entire trees. Wisteria hung over the driveway in an arch, making for a jaw-dropping entrance to the old estate. There was even a stream that ran through the property, with wisteria hanging over the stone bridge and cascading towards the water.

Since it was now January and winter, all the purple blossoms had been pruned by the gardener, leaving only the vines.

Still, the Wisteria Estate was a sight to behold. Turning off the ignition of the mint green VW, Bell took a deep breath. Today was her first day. She crossed her fingers that it would go well. She was wearing what she thought was the perfect first day outfit—a black turtleneck, back and white high-waist plaid skirt, black tights, pointy toe black over-the-knee boots with a slight kitten heel, and the pièce de résistance...her bright pink saddlebag that she had bought especially for the occasion. Every piece of her brightly highlighted hair had been curled and sprayed it into submission.

"Be good," she had told Georgia before leaving. "The dog walker will be in at noon." Before arriving in Pink Shell Shores, she had conducted a Skype-interview with a well-reviewed dog walking service in town. She had left her key for the dog walker under a giant shell in her front-yard.

Her hands shook as she locked her car and fumbled around in her purse for her lip-gloss, which she applied in copious amounts. Precisely ten minutes early for her nine o'clock start, Bell marveled and knew this was meant to be as she passed by a restored antique light pink truck—a 1930s Ford Model A parked prominently on the circular driveway. She walked up the marble stairs and pushed open the heavy double doors.

If the outside had tugged at her heartstrings, the interior of the Wisteria Estate was a full-blown heart stopper. She held up her hand to her mouth to hide her surprise, her eyes like saucers.

Recently re-designed by a Milan-based interior designer, the lobby of the Wisteria Estate now had flamingo pink walls, oversized white and pink crystal chandeliers, black-and-white marble flooring, contemporary frescos painted in gelato colors into the mile-high ceilings, gold gilded mirrors everywhere, and a giant gold front desk with the largest vase Bell had ever seen—of course, it was overflowing with wisteria.

The re-design, touted by some as gaudy and others as genius, had proved to be a major revenue generator. The once understated and under-the-radar hotel had become the "it-spot" for Instagrammers, influencers, brides, and bloggers. The Wisteria Estate had been booked to full capacity for weddings and events since the re-design. If her opinion counted for anything, it was the singularly most beautiful, magical place Bell had ever stepped into. It was like an alternate reality. This was already a million times better than the stuffy atmosphere she had grown accustomed to at the Saint Thomas Hotel. Of course, now that she wasn't going to see Nigel anymore, it was already loads better...

"Can I help you?"

Bell snapped back to the present moment. The words came from a nice looking man, about her age, with a stylishly cropped and slicked back hairstyle. He wore all black and had exceptionally shiny shoes.

"I hope so. I'm here for my first day of work. My name is Bell. Aribella Lacroix. But I go by Bell. I'm the new wedding and venue coordinator. I was told to ask for Harlow?"

If Bell had observed correctly, she was certain she had seen the corner of the man's mouth twitch. "I'm Mark. It's nice to meet you. Feel free to take a seat. I'll let her know you're here." He pointed towards an overstuffed ivory velvet sofa behind her, where she took a seat after she had thanked him.

Already, Bell was feeling like she had more than made the right decision. She breathed a sigh of relief. Sometimes, the universe seemed to have it all worked out.

"Aribella? You're late."

Harlow Williams was walking towards her, looking immaculate in a white suit with a black lacy shirt beneath, bright red lips, brighter red stilettos, and even brighter coiffed red hair. Harlow glanced at her iPad between steps, before stopping in front of Bell and shaking her hand.

Bell's heart sank. "I'm—I'm so sorry," she fumbled as heat built in her cheeks. She could have sworn that the email said nine o'clock. "I thought I was supposed to be here for nine –"

Harlow burst out into peels of energetic laughter. "I was just kidding. You're right on time. What a way to start a new job though, huh? It's a rush!"

In ten minutes, Bell had learned that Harlow Williams was a fast-talker, fast-walker, high-energy, manager extraordinaire. Barely able to keep up, Bell seemed to jog beside her new boss, Harlow, who did everything at a faster speed. As they toured the estate, Bell learned that Harlow had been responsible for convincing Randy Coulter, the owner of the Wisteria Estate, to go ahead with the revamp. In the two short years she had come on as manager at the Wisteria, as she called it, Harlow had completely turned it around. She wasn't afraid to say so, either.

"Let me tell you, we've been looking for someone like you. Someone with energy. Zest." Harlow continued talking a mile-a-minute. "The last venue coordinator..." Harlow pulled a face. "...*borrrrrrrring*. It was like she hadn't looked at a Pinterest board in her life. At every event it was tea roses, tea roses, tea roses. I mean, tea roses are nice and all, but they're not going to get a wedding featured on the cover of a magazine, are they?"

Bell pulled a sympathetic face. She made a mental note never to use tea roses. "I suppose not, no."

"Right?"

"Absolutely." The apples of Bell's cheeks hurt from all the smiling.

It became clear to Bell that Harlow liked enthusiasm. Of course, no matter how much coffee she consumed, she could never match the infectious energy that seemed naturally abundant in Harlow. Bell got a complete tour of the Wisteria—from the art deco inspired stairwells clad in bright pink and mint-green wallpaper, to the pink-everywhere lounge with a sky-light, where everything from the zigzag carpet to the plush sofas to the chandelier was pink, and finally to the bar area. Bell's heart fluttered as she took it all in, feeling in awe and completely at a loss for words, which was fine because Harlow seemed to have a lot to say anyway. Although she had her iPhone ready to take notes, so far she hadn't recorded a single thing. She breathlessly took it all in.

Harlow insisted that the two of them take a quick break at the bar—a room that was uncharacteristically mint-green and had gold accents. Her eyes darted upwards where the architect had managed to sneak in a hint of pink... on the ceiling. Harry Connick Junior crooned over the sound system.

"Now that we have looked around, I can see from your expression that you feel the same way about this place as I do," Harlow said.

Bell felt like Alice down the rabbit hole. After being in this hotel, how would anything else ever measure up? Before she had a chance to respond, Harlow was already onto the next topic. In the middle of the room was a circular bar where mixologists shook fancy drinks in copper cocktail shakers. Bell perched beside Harlow on her velvet barstool, while a handsome looking bartender wearing a pink sweater with the sleeves pushed up, revealing various tattoos, was making pastel-colored mixed drinks.

"Terence, would you mind rustling up whatever leftover champagne we have from last night's event? And two glasses?"

Harlow asked, her clipped tones becoming syrupy-sweet as she turned to him.

Terence gave an almost imperceptible wink towards Harlow, who glanced at Bell and winked in her direction.

Harlow leaned in towards her. "What's the point in being a party planner if you can't celebrate yourself once in awhile, right?"

She did her best to quell the excitement bubbling inside her. Champagne? At lunch? On her first day? As she glanced at her watch, she did her best to hide her surprise that almost half of the day had already passed while they were looking through the estate. Terence placed the crystal glasses in front of them and expertly uncorked a bottle of champagne, filling their glasses. Harlow smiled as she held up her glass to Bell.

"Cheers. To our new wedding and venue coordinator."

Bell clinked her glass with Harlow's, feeling herself flushing on the first sip. Her excitement rose like the bubbles in her glass.

"Harlow, thank you so much. This has been an unforgettable first day. I'm so excited to get started with the events that need planning," she said.

Harlow placed drink on the marble countertop and leaned in towards Bell, lowering her voice. "As the wedding and venue coordinator, you're going to be the head honcho for all major events." Harlow's eyes were wide and suddenly serious. "You understand the importance of this, I'm sure? We have a certain aesthetic. A certain reputation to uphold. What I'm going to say is incredibly important. Everything. Must. Run. Smoothly."

A lump formed in Bell's throat, which she swallowed. She nodded. Bell wanted to clarify that, of course, minor hiccups were to be expected? But Harlow didn't give the impression that any mistakes were made around here. Under Harlow's watch, the Wisteria Estate was a tightly run ship. And it was steered towards unparalleled success.

Bell took a nervous gulp of her champagne and forced a smile, hoping she looked more confident than she felt.

"Of course. I won't let you down," she said, a slight tremble in her voice.

Harlow didn't seem to notice. "Wonderful! Well, cheers to that. Now, lets go over the details more closely..."

The first day of work passed in a flash of pink, gold, and mint green. The two glasses of champagne at lunch had certainly helped. Bell felt exhilarated, exhausted, and ready to get home to Georgia. She was eager to see how the new dog walker, Sam, had worked out. She knew that Georgia could be fussy about who she was walked with. After saying a quick goodbye to Harlow, who by the end of the day hadn't felt quite as intimidating, Bell had managed to leave only a half hour after her scheduled finish time. After all, she wanted to leave a good impression.

As she stepped outside, she sighed a huge sigh of relief. The day had been a success. More than a success – it had been *perfect*. Her whole body tensed as she thought back to Harlow's words.

Everything. Must. Run. Smoothly.

Surely everything would, Bell reassured herself. Coming from Boston, it hadn't registered as strange to Bell that snowdrifts had started forming.

"Be careful on your drive home!" Mark said as she passed him to the parking lot. "We've gotten a little flash storm. Roads are awful!"

Bell suppressed the urge to smile. "Thank you, I'm sure I'll be fine. I'll see you tomorrow!" she said pleasantly. She was coming from Boston. People in Pink Shell Shores were clearly unaccustomed to a bit of snow.

The snow was coming down heavily, and Bell had to use the snowbrush to clear off the thick layer of snow that had made itself at home on the roof. By the end, she found herself panting slightly, cheeks flushed, and feet frozen. She couldn't wait to get home to a nice cup of hot chocolate. Or perhaps something stronger.

Hopping inside her car, she revved up the reliable old engine, throwing it a little too fast into reverse, and set off back home. Bell turned on the radio and sang along her favorite early nineties Madonna songs. She felt her shoulders ease.

Not knowing Pink Shell Shores very well, Bell relied on her iPhone's navigation system. As she gripped her steering wheel, the snow was falling even harder, and had her wiper blades on full-speed to try to maintain her visibility. She turned up her anti-fog to full-blast, but it barely made a difference.

She was only ten minutes away from home when her car began skidding on the ice-covered roads. Gripping the wheel, her stomach lurched as the car skidded again before straightening out. Her father, a retired firefighter, had always warned her against driving in these conditions. "When the snow sits on top of the ice, I know we're going to have a busy night at the station." Bell wished she could have taken his advice to stay home in these driving conditions, but now it was too late. She gripped the steering wheel as tightly as she ever had and she felt the torque of her car losing control, skidding along the black ice. Her pounding heart dropped into her stomach as she let out a cry of frustration.

Thunk.

In a split second, her car had veered off the road into a snowbank. In all her years of driving, she had never so much as put a scratch on her car. With her heart still racing, one hand holding the wheel, Bell put it into reverse, popped the clutch, while simultaneously slamming down the gas pedal. Her car made a pathetic gurgling sound, puttering, before it stopped responding to her attempts entirely. The engine light flashed, and Bell let out a groan that could have reached her aunt in Nantucket. The wind whipped at her car, making the whole car shake. It left her with an empty feeling in the pit of her stomach.

She checked her phone, which had a spotty signal and five percent battery left on it. Today of all days, she had forgotten her charger at home. She didn't want to waste a phone call on a towing company, especially if they didn't respond. Worst of all, she thought with a hint of panic; she didn't know where she was, so it would be hard to tell them where they should rescue her.

Bell tried to take a calming breath, but it came out as more of a shudder. Her father's words echoed in her mind. "Always have a blanket, a shovel, and a lamp in your vehicle emergency kit." Bell gulped. She had had those things, but removed them for the move from Boston. What if no one came? What if she had to spend the night in her car? She looked around at the light grey fabric seats. Surely they wouldn't be able to insulate her from freezing to death.

Before she knew what she was doing, Bell took off one of her kitten-heeled boots. She stretched her mitten over her sock-clad foot as protection against the cold and set out. *I'm not going to die in a snowstorm during my first day on the job*, Bell thought. Opening the door, she hopped on one leg towards the icy snow bank where the car was parked and she chipped away at it with her shoe.

"Take that! And that!" she cried out to the universe, hoping at any second that the frozen mound of snow would shrink and free her car from the snowdrift. Her fingers numbed, the frigid winds made her wince as it bristled against her exposed skin on her face. After what felt like ages, the snow bank actually looked *bigger*. Plus, her foot was now freezing cold, numb, and had developed an uncomfortable tingling sensation.

Bell had not woken up that morning thinking about the possible loss of a foot. Ironically, she was looking forward to leaving this kind of weather behind in Boston when she moved. Here it was. Had it followed her to Pink Shell Shores? Morosely, she hobbled back towards her car. She couldn't push the car out of the snow bank—it wouldn't budge—and she certainly couldn't pull it herself. Her heart thudded in her chest as a cold sinking feeling came over her. Sitting again in the driver's seat, Bell blinked back hot tears.

I'm not going to cry, she told herself. *I have to figure this out.*

As she felt like the situation was hopeless, lights from an upcoming car lit the snowy road ahead. Before she had a second to think, Bell instinctively jumped out the car door, one boot still in hand. She began waving her arms.

"Over here!" She didn't even know if she could be heard with the howl of the winds. But she didn't care. She had to get this driver's attention. As the car drew nearer, she felt her heartbeat returning to a normal pace as the driver slowed to a stop. The driver of the light blue vintage Chevrolet truck rolled down his window.

"You look like you could use a hand," he said easily. "That's a nice car, but it doesn't look like it's going anywhere soon."

Bell had never felt so relieved to see a pickup truck in her entire life. She beamed back at the man. "Oh my gosh, yes. Thank you so much. My car got stuck," she yelled over the blustering winds.

"So I take it that's a yes?"

"Yes! That would be so helpful. I just need some help getting this thing out of the snow bank." Bell didn't care who he was or what he did. At that moment, she would have accepted help from anyone. She was now cold, exhausted, and wanted to get home.

He looked from the boot in her hand to the mitten covering her bare foot.

"I'm not crazy," Bell added, before realizing saying that had the unfortunate effect of making her seem more ridiculous. She sat back down in her car and pulled her boot back on.

The driver pulled his truck over to the side of the narrow road, and after putting on his hazard lights, came over to assess the damage.

"What on earth are you doing? Trying to get hypothermia?" he asked.

Bell, now standing beside her car, stood up as straight and dignified as possible. "Actually," she began. "I was using my resources at hand to try to dig myself out."

"With your boot?" He didn't sound convinced.

Bell nodded as he took a few steps around to assess the car, Bell couldn't help but notice him. Broad shoulders and cut jawline. Bell wondered if this man's father was an old cowboy? Maybe a model for Marlboro Cigarettes?

Bell stood off to the side, looking for passing cars. She wouldn't want anyone to get into another accident with their respective stopped cars. Plus, standing off to the side meant that she could take a better look at him. Or, if he turned out to be a murderer, she would have a head start running away. The man motioned for her to come over. Abandoning her murderer fears, Bell walked over, feeling her cheeks flush both at the cold and the sight of him.

"I would try to help you push it out of this snow bank," he began. "But it's not going to be much use. See here? That's why it probably wasn't moving much when you pushed it. I assume you tried to push it before you started chiseling away at the snow?"

Bell could only bring herself to nod, feeling her cheeks becoming hot. He brought her around the corner where he pointed towards her front tire. It was completely deflated. Her face fell and she could feel a lump rising in her throat.

"Oh my gosh. I need to get home and take Georgia for a walk," she blurted out. She was shivering now, and could feel herself rambling as her panic rose. "It's her first day at home alone. My dog, Georgia. She's a rescue, and kind of temperamental and nervous. We just moved here, and this was my first day at work away from her."

Now that she was closer, she could fully see the man's features. Strong jaw, sure, but even more noticeable up close was the intensity of his gaze.

"I'm guessing you don't work as a mechanic," he ventured, looking down at her kitten heel boots that were getting destroyed by the snow. For the first time in this whole situation, Bell laughed. "Come on," he said. "I'll give you a lift. You can call a tow truck on the way, if you like."

Bell nodded, feeling the lump in her throat dissipate. "Thank you. Thank you so much."

The man nodded once and walked back to his truck, opening up the side door for her. "The doors on this truck are a bit finicky too. Like your Georgia," he said with a smile, revealing a set of even teeth. Bell's stomach swooped as she laughed, but this time it came out all high pitched and squeaky.

"Thanks," Bell said between chattering teeth. She admired the tan leather bucket seats as she stepped into the car, feeling herself relax. She was on her way to see Georgia. Everything would be okay.

"This is a *really* nice truck," she said, looking around. He stepped into the driver's seat and revved the engine. Soul revival music blared over his speaker system, and his hand flew to the volume dial to turn it down. "It's my first time in a Chevy Cameo Carrier. When were they made—the fifties?"

He nodded. "Yeah, this is a '57 model. Chevrolet stopped making them the following year so the parts are hard to find.

"The car's a lot of work then, I suppose?" she asked conversationally. Vintage cars made everyday feel special. She couldn't figure out why. It was why she would rather spend a few thousand dollars every year keeping the Superbeetle rolling along rather than trade it in for some brand new model. To her, it was all about the joy she got riding along. It meant more to her than practicalities any day.

Bell swore she saw a flash of sadness across his otherwise relaxed and contented face. "Yeah. It's a lot of work, sure. But to me, it's worth it."

He turned on the heater at full blast, which felt like balm on scorched skin. Even her foot began to slowly regain feeling. He asked Bell for her address, which she punched into his phone GPS.

"Fourteen Oyster Lane. It's not too far from here."

He nodded, turning the truck around in the snow. "I know the street. Should get you there in ten minutes. And by then, there's a good chance you still might reach Hank."

"Hank?"

"The mechanic."

"As in, *singular*?"

He laughed, which sent a trill of flutters through Bell's stomach. "You really haven't been here long, have you? Yeah, there's just one mechanic in town."

"So you must be from Pink Shell Shores?"

"In a way. I spent a lot of time here growing up. It's my home away from home. I come down here whenever I can."

Bell's interest piqued. "So you're not here as much as you'd like?" she couldn't help but ask.

"Nope."

She was expecting more of an answer, but she didn't want to pry. Before she knew it, they were pulling onto Oyster Lane.

"Well, this is me," Bell said as they pulled in front of her house. "Thank you so, so much. Honestly, you saved me back there. I don't know what I would have done."

He laughed. "Oh, I have a feeling you would've been alright. That, or you would've lost a toe." A tiny, almost imperceptible giggle escaped from the otherwise serious man. It was closely followed by another. Before Bell knew it, he was full on clutching at his sides, gasping for air, which made Bell laugh.

"I'm sorry, I'm just teasing," he said, wiping his eyes. "That's got to be the best attempt at snow removal I've seen yet. Besides, this town's full of friendly faces. Someone would have come along eventually."

"Seriously though, thank you." Bell looked to her house, where she knew Georgia was waiting for her. "I'd better get going. It was nice meeting you, uh..."

She paused, realizing she didn't yet know his name.

"Colt," he said, extending a hand.

"Well, nice to meet you, Colt. And thank you for the drive."

She waited momentarily, wondering if he might suggest seeing her again. She had surreptitiously checked his left hand—no ring, and the car was void of any signs of a woman's presence. But he gave her a kind smile.

"Anytime," he said easily.

"Okay, bye!" she said, giving him one final chance. When he said nothing, she stepped out of the car and he drove away with the purr of his engine. Bell ran inside, her foot aching, and was greeted immediately upon opening the door by a delighted Georgia, who ran around in circles and promptly peed on the floor from excitement.

"Tomorrow is always another day," she said to Georgia, who trailed at her feet as she walked to the kitchen to grab a roll of paper towels. Even still, at that moment there was no place Bell would rather have been—at home with Georgia.

Chapter Three

By the next morning, the snow from the wayward storm had turned to slush and Pink Shell Shores had returned to its balmy winter temperature. Bell felt like she had already met half the town. Bright and early, she had called Hank the local auto mechanic. He would drive her to work before going to grab her car. She crossed her fingers it was still there and hadn't already been towed.

The night before, Bell had a restless sleep that was made worse by Georgia's unrelenting snores. Bell couldn't help but allow Georgia to take up the other half of her queen-sized bed. Besides, no one else was using it. Up at the crack of dawn, Bell let Georgia out in the backyard, put kibble in Georgia's bowl, made a pot of coffee, let Georgia back inside, and finally made breakfast for herself. First grabbing a slice of bread and smearing it with hazelnut spread, Bell settled down on the couch with her plate.

Georgia came over hopped onto the couch, nuzzling her head on Bell's knee.

"You can't have any," Bell told Georgia, who looked wistfully at the hazelnut spread. "It has chocolate in it. And chocolate is no good for dogs."

Outside the window, the snow had stopped falling and the skies had cleared. It looked like it was destined to be a beautiful day. After getting dressed in a pair of black and white gingham pants, a white floaty top, and a pair of white booties that she thought looked perfect with her pants, Bell gave Georgia a walk around the block two times before grabbing her purse for work.

"I'll see you soon Georgia!"

It was seven o'clock, and the sun had barely cast its rays in the sky. Just like he said, Hank pulled up in his truck at seven sharp. He waved to her as she walked over.

"Hiya, Aribella is it?" Hank stepped out of his truck and shook her hand. In his late forties, she guessed, he was handsome and affable with a wide grin and a thermos of coffee.

"Bell, you can call me Bell." She had forgotten how abrupt she could sound when she had only had one cup of coffee, as she stifled a yawn.

Hank nodded. "Alright then. Bell it is. Now, let's get you this car of yours."

Hank drove her to the site where her car was parked. As it turned out, Hank had already passed it by the evening before, and had told Bell not to worry. He had seen worse. By the time they got there, to Bell's relief the car was still there.

Hank laughed. "You didn't need to worry so much. I've seen cars in the ditch sit there for months before someone decides that they are going to do something about it."

He towed her car and dropped her off at the Wisteria Estate with just enough time for her to get to work a full hour early. And so, after waving goodbye to Hank—who promised to drop off her fully repaired car in the parking lot of the Wisteria Estate by the end of the day—Bell walked to work. She expected it to be a peaceful, serene place to collect her thoughts before the day started. Out of the corner of her eye, she saw a familiar truck in the parking lot as she walked up the steps.

As she opened the door to the Wisteria, her jaw dropped. "Colt?"

Colt stood in the lobby looking even more handsome than the day before. He was talking to Mark and brandishing a piece of paper. *Probably an itemized bill*, Bell thought. Strange that he hadn't mentioned he was a guest at the hotel.

For the briefest of instances, it flashed through Bell's mind that perhaps he was there to see her. Perhaps he *was*.

"Hi," she said, her heart pounding as she walked up to him. She gave Mark a friendly wave.

As Colt turned in her direction, the flicker of recognition crossed his face. "Oh, hi! That's right. You work here. That's right."

Perhaps he *wasn't*.

Her heart sank, and she did her best to hide her disappointment with a bright smile as she nodded. She wanted to ask him if he was a guest at the hotel, but the way he kept shooting nervous glances at Mark, it made Bell wonder if he preferred to be left alone.

She opened her mouth to say she ought to be going when Mark piped in. "Harlow is already upstairs in her office, if you wanted to pop in," he suggested helpfully. Bell flashed him a grateful smile.

"Thanks, Mark. That's exactly what I'll do." She glanced at Colt one more time, feeling a swoop in her stomach. *So he might be a guest here. But that doesn't mean he doesn't want to see me.* "Nice to run into you again, Colt. I hope to see you around soon."

Colt gave the briefest of nods, before turning back towards Mark and continuing their discussion. As she walked up the staircase, she caught him glancing in her direction, and she nervously looked away as butterflies filled her stomach.

She couldn't shake that feeling all the way up the stairs, beaming as she knocked carefully on the door to Harlow's office. She heard a muffled "Come in!"

Bell pushed open the door, unprepared for what was happening in front of her.

"Uh, would you like me to come back at a better time?" Bell ventured. In the middle of the room lay a white yoga mat, with Harlow clad entirely in red yoga gear and a full face of makeup. She was posed in a headstand.

Bell couldn't remember the last time she had managed to catch a yoga class, let alone bring her yoga gear to work.

"Nonsense," Harlow said, kicking down one leg at a time, before sitting crossed legged in the middle of her office. "Come on in!"

Bell walked in, tentatively taking a seat on a clear acrylic chair with the fluffy salmon-pink pillow that was more for aesthetic purposes than for comfort. She shifted, trying to find a position that didn't make her back ache.

"Do you have a yoga practice? I would *die* without yoga," Harlow said emphatically, this time supporting herself against the wall before kicking up each leg, so she was in another headstand.

"Uh, no. Not really. But I jog!" Bell said in a moment of inspiration. It wasn't that far a stretch from the truth. She *could* jog. She had *thought* about taking up jogging, after all. And what were all of those walks with Georgia if not a cardiovascular workout?

"You should bring your mat sometime," Harlow offered, gracefully coming out of the supported headstand and finding her way to her desk.

Wide-eyed, Bell nodded, already thinking of a list of possible excuses. "Definitely!"

"Now, getting down to business," Harlow said, suddenly shifting into a business-like tone and taking on an entirely different persona. "We have a pretty major wedding coming up. It's supposed to get us a lot of media coverage. Apparently, the bride has big plans. And you're going to be their first point of contact, as the wedding and venue coordinator on site. Of course, I'm always available to help," she added.

This had been more what Bell had expected. She grabbed her notepad from her new purse and began taking notes.

"Right. The Valentine's Day wedding," Bell said, remembering what Harlow had mentioned it to her yesterday.

"Now, the last wedding coordinator. Like I told you," Harlow said, leaning in and lowering her voice. "She just wasn't up to speed for such a big wedding."

A lump in Bell's throat developed. She sure hoped that she could cut it. At her old job, she had been the most in demand wedding coordinator at the Saint Thomas hotel. All the couples wanted *her* to plan their big day. Not only did she bring a huge dose of enthusiasm, Bell had pulled off some of the most extravagant weddings that Boston hotel had seen—some even featured in high-end bridal magazines. Needless to say, her portfolio was outstanding.

Bell smoothed an invisible wrinkle on her blouse and took a deep breath to steady herself. "What does the couple have in mind, if you don't mind my asking?"

She braced herself for a ludicrous response. She had heard it all. Hot air balloons that would descend into the garden in the back of the hotel. New Year's Eve weddings where everyone was given candles to hold as the bride and groom said their I Do's. A Christmas Eve wedding where everyone, including the bride, wore red and green.

"Well," Harlow began, looking hesitant. "They want their Valentine's Day wedding to have pink everything. Which, of course, you've seen our decor." Harlow laughed. "It's a natural fit."

Bell frowned. "Pink everything? Well, that's not so bad." She felt the knot in her stomach unclench.

Harlow's face lit up. "Oh, that's not it. No, no."

The worst ran through Bell's mind. "It's not a... a nudist wedding, is it?" she asked as tactfully as she could.

Luckily, Harlow burst into peals of laughter, before catching her breath. "No, no. Nothing like that. Gosh, that would be hilarious. But we don't do things like that here."

Bell's cheeks burned. *Obviously* the Wisteria Estate didn't have nudist weddings. She could have kicked herself. "Of course. Right," she said.

"It's the *bride* that's the problem," Harlow explained. "Not the theme."

Bell nodded, taking notes. She had come across her fair share of bridezillas, who she generally thought got a bad rap. After all, they only wanted a perfect day.

Harlow continued. "She has fired three caterers in town, including the one here at the Wisteria Estate. She has gone through the two florists in town and proclaimed that the limousine company isn't up to speed."

Bell frowned, her mind whirling into problem-solving mode. "Okay. So what *has* she chosen?"

Harlow shrugged. "The dress? I don't know. She was hard on the last girl in your position. You've got your work cut out for you with this one."

Nodding, Bell looked up from her notes. "So, from what you are telling me, practically nothing has been done and just to clarify, the wedding is in six weeks?" she asked incredulously. From what it sounded like, Bell had an entire wedding to plan.

In six weeks.

It wasn't possible. It simply wasn't possible. Bell took a steadying breath.

Harlow laughed. "I told you, you've got your work cut out for you." Harlow's phone lit up across the desk, and as she glanced at the screen, she looked immediately distracted. "So, you'll be meeting with the happy couple shortly. Consider this wedding your full-time gig until the next one. Of course, I'll brief you on everything beforehand. But this Valentine's Day wedding is your one and only job. Make this wedding a hit, and I can promise you, it won't go unnoticed."

Bell smiled, hoping she was effectively hiding the creeping concern that rose in her chest. "Don't worry," she said, laughing a little too hard. "I'll take care of everything."

Shaking off the nerves that crept up, Bell prepared for her meeting with the couple. Only ten minutes until she met the famous—or *infamous*—bride. How bad could she be?

Today, Bell was set up her own office. A plaque outside the door was even being made with her name on it. A shiver of anticipation ran through her at the thought. She couldn't wait to make this place *hers*. Unlike the rest of the Wisteria Estate, Bell's office was beige and dreary. No splashes of pink anywhere. She sat at a bare wood desk. Wisteria vines hung over ancient glass window panes, obstructing her view of the gardens. It was clear that the last person who held that position hadn't taken a shine to the venues updated decor. She would have to remedy that soon.

"Knock knock?"

Bell turned to see a perky-looking woman walking into her office. The woman wore large sunglasses, despite that they were indoors, and carried with her a handbag that Bell knew cost five figures. Without so much as a hair out of place, this was certainly the bride that Harlow had warned her about. Bell's stomach flip-flopped as the woman gave her a wide smile and sat across from her.

Bell took a deep breath to steady herself. She was a professional. She could handle any difficult client who came her way. Even if they looked like they had walked straight out of a magazine.

"You must be –" Bell began, suddenly freezing. Harlow had never told her the client's name. Or perhaps she had. Either way, Bell was drawing a blank.

Polite as she was pretty, the woman smiled. "Margaret. But everyone calls me Maggie. Maggie Blazer. It's nice to meet you."

Maggie reached out a manicured hand to shake Bell's. She felt about three feet tall.

"Right, of course. Momentary brain glitch," Bell laughed. "It's so nice to finally meet you Maggie. I can't *wait* to begin making your wedding dreams a reality."

Maggie smoothed the skirt of her dress, looking satisfied. "That's just what I like to hear. The last girl in your position..." Maggie rolled her eyes, making Bell laugh nervously. She *wanted* Maggie to like her. She *needed* Maggie to like her. This was her first client. Her only chance to make a first impression in this new job. She was determined to make her new life in Pink Shell Shores a success.

"Don't worry, I'll work around the clock to make sure we get it all ready in time," Bell said. Maggie's eyes lit up, and Bell wondered if she had said something she shouldn't. As she opened her mouth to speak, a knock on the door interrupted them.

"Colt!" Maggie scolded. "You're late."

Bell could have melted right into her chair. With wide eyes, Bell watched Colt walk into the small office. He looked equally stunned to see her sitting across from his fiancé.

Maggie rolled her eyes again. "Okay, Colt. Rude of you not to introduce yourself. Like I told you. Remember?" Maggie's attention snapped back to Bell, and she smiled sweetly. "We're working on etiquette," she said with a wink.

Bell, still at a loss for words, nodded. "Right. Great. You can never be too polite," she managed, her throat feeling tight. Now it made sense why he was at the reception desk. He wasn't there to see her. He was there to plan his wedding. *To Maggie.*

"It's nice to see you again you, Bell," Colt said, reaching out to shake Bell's hand.

Maggie's head swiveled to Bell, her eyes narrowing. "You know each other?"

"Bell's the person I gave a ride to. When her car broke down," Colt said, taking a seat beside Maggie.

"You didn't tell me that person was a *she*," Maggie muttered. She had on a sour expression that perked up only as Colt reached over to hold her hand.

Bell's heart was pounding. The tension in the room could be cut with a knife. "Okay, well. It's so nice to meet you both officially and in person." She had a huge fake smile plastered on her face she hoped did the trick at masking her anxiety. "Shall we get started?"

Over an hour passed and Maggie continued to talk about what she wanted for her Valentine's Day wedding, which was *six weeks away*. Changing the wedding coordinator at such a last minute was tricky in the best of scenarios. Let alone, with an inflexible bride who seemed to be particular about everything.

"So, you want doves released after the vows?" Bell echoed, typing away. She wiped her brow.

"Not just doves. Doves and *swans*," Maggie countered. Colt checked his phone for the umpteenth time.

"Right." Bell frowned. She took her fingers off the keyboard. "See, the thing is, I'm not sure swans are guaranteed to fly with the doves like you're imagining." Bell had worked with swans in the past. As her favorite animal, she knew they required respect and distance. They certainly wouldn't fly out of a cage upon command.

Maggie pouted. "Colt, tell her I want swans."

Colt exhaled, looking up from his phone. "I think this is a great place to finish today," he said crisply. "We've got someone who can sort out most of the details."

Bell could feel a migraine threatening, and she stood up quickly. "Well, we want to make sure that all of these details are done with care and quality. Let's take a few days, I'll call the vendors and see what I can do, and we can reconvene?"

"No," Maggie said, her eyes narrowing. "I want to meet tomorrow."

Bell's eyebrows shot up. "Tomorrow?"

"Yes. Tomorrow." Maggie remained seated, her arms crossed.

The words of Harlow echoed in Bell's mind. *Everything must run smoothly.*

Bell took a deep breath, just as Colt began to protest. "No, no. It's fine," she said, trying to sound cheerful. "Tomorrow works great."

Maggie's expression immediately brightened. "Oh Bell. You're such a star."

Bell felt a little shaky as she walked them out. "All part of the Wisteria Estate experience. Do you two have anything lovely planned for the rest of the day?"

"High tea at Tea Reading," Maggie said, screwing up her face. "It's nothing like Alice's Tea Cup in Manhattan."

"Yes, well, we're not in Manhattan," Colt said in an unreadable tone.

"Sourpuss. He's just sad that I don't like Pink Shell Shores as much as him. It's where his family has vacationed forever. Me, I prefer the Hamptons."

Bell nodded, unsure of what to say. "Right. Well, enjoy!"

After Colt and Maggie had left, Bell collapsed into her desk chair and reviewed Maggie's so-called *essentials* for the wedding. Where was she going to find swans that would fly on cue? How was she going to find three hundred crystal champagne flutes with the name of each guest engraved into the crystal? Would she find another florist near Pink Shell Shores who could conjure up fifty bouquets of pink orchids? Could pink orchids even be ordered on such short notice? Would Maggie's bridesmaids agree to having their hair highlighted the same honey blonde shade? Maggie had seemed oblivious to these concerns when Bell raised them during their appointment.

"Knock knock?"

Bell stiffened, but relaxed as soon as she saw that it was Harlow. "Oh, hi!" She tried to sound bright, but she could feel her energy waning.

"I thought you might like a coffee," Harlow offered, placing a china teacup filled to the brim. "I didn't know how you took it," she said, proffering a series of sugar packets.

Bell took a grateful sip. "It's perfect. Thanks Harlow."

Harlow sat on Bell's desk, cocking one eyebrow. "So, how'd it go?"

Bell considered telling Harlow the truth. That Maggie seemed to have some unrealistic expectations for her wedding. Instead, Bell smiled.

"Oh, no problem at all. I'll manage."

Harlow looked like she didn't know whether to believe her, but chose not to press her further. "Alright, want to meet after work today for a drink today? Don't worry, it's on me," Harlow added with a wink.

She didn't know how Harlow did it—from yoga, to being a mom of a three-year-old daughter (Harlow had mentioned this in their first meeting), to managing a social life.

"Yes," Bell breathed a sigh of relief. "That sounds like exactly what I need."

The rest of the day flew by. Bell had been on hold with an engraver for a half hour before being told no–they didn't do engraving on crystal flutes. She had even called the local zoo—no, they didn't do animal rentals—in addition to every service that provided dove releases. None of them had even *heard* of doing it with a swan. One vendor straight up laughed. Going round in circles, Bell felt like she was about to go crazy when the clock struck five. She hadn't even touched base with the florists. Seconds later, Harlow showed up at her door.

"Ready?"

The pair of them headed downstairs towards the bar. It was already filling up with the after-work crowd. Terence was known for making a killer cocktail, and the bar and adjacent dining room in the Wisteria Estate was a popular dinner spot. Locals and tourists alike were streaming in, filling up the marble-clad tables and taking pictures for their Instagram accounts.

Pulling up a seat at the bar, Bell was about to unload about her day when she did a double take. Was that Maggie sitting at the bar?

"Hey, is that who I think it is?" Bell whispered to Harlow, who was already perusing the drinks menu.

Harlow looked up and rolled her eyes. "She's probably doing a drinks sampling. Making sure everything is *exactly* how she wants it."

"Yeah, that must be it," Bell said absently. Maggie still hadn't seen them. Bell watched as Maggie flagged down Terence and ordered another drink from him with a flirtatious grin.

Harlow continued. "Not that there's anything wrong with being a perfectionist. But it's knowing when to let up!"

Bell nodded, only half-listening. She kept sneaking glances towards Maggie, who was now laughing uncontrollably at something Terence had said.

"I would say tell me everything, but..." Harlow continued, jutting her chin in Maggie's direction.

Bell laughed. "No, that's all right. There's not much to report anyway."

The two of them ordered their drinks from another bartender. Terence had remained firmly planted in front of Maggie since they arrived. As soon as their drinks arrived, Harlow clinked hers against Bell's.

"Cheers. To getting through the tough days and thriving on the good ones."

Bell smiled. She couldn't imagine truer words. She also couldn't imagine that Maggie was getting married to Colt, as she observed Maggie leaning over the bar countertop to poke Terence in the chest with a wide grin. No, she couldn't imagine that one bit.

Chapter Four

Georgia and Bell trotted down Oyster Lane. Inside Bell's head felt like a NASA operating system. Even though it was Saturday, she couldn't stop thinking about work. Had she confirmed with the florist? Would the chair cover company switch the order from bright white to ivory? When were the votive and candle company going to call her back about changing the setup? The pressure was getting to Bell. Another day ticked off and now the Valentine's Day wedding was *less* than six weeks away. This particular day was turning into a nightmare.

Weddings sure had changed since Bell began working in the industry ten years earlier. Brides used to be satisfied with a nice wedding. Now, it seemed like everything was about making the wedding as Pinterest-worthy as possible. Not that it was necessarily such a bad thing, but Bell had watched countless brides have meltdowns about the pressure they put on themselves.

Maggie was different. She had already called Bell six times, and counting, since their last meeting. Bell had only given Maggie her cell phone number for emergencies. She hadn't realized that Maggie's version of what qualified as an emergency would be so drastically different from her own.

Bell felt a tug at the leash and her attention was jolted back to the present moment. Georgia was craning her neck, trying to reach a nearby squirrel.

"Bell!"

Bell turned to see Colt, exiting from one of the opulent estates on Oyster Lane. A warm feeling spread all over. That's when it all went fuzzy.

"Georgia, *nooooooo!*"

The leash slithered out of Bell's hand as Georgia made a break for it. From the corner of her eye, Bell saw a car slowly driving down Oyster Lane. Georgia was dashing across the street without a care in the world as the squirrel ran towards a tree in Colt's front yard. Bell had never run so fast in her life. Her lungs ached as she screamed to Georgia to stop. She held up her hand to the oncoming driver who slowed to a stop.

Frantically, Bell looked from the driver to Georgia. In an instant, everything was calm again. Georgia was now sitting at Colt's feet, firmly in his grasp. She exhaled a sigh of relief, feeling her knees buckle beneath her.

"Georgia. You scared me," she breathed.

Colt extended a hand to Georgia, who licked away at his palm. Colt wore a jacket and hat, his cheeks rosy from the cold. Looking concerned, Colt peered at Bell. "You alright?"

Georgia leaned against the tree to steady herself. The squirrel was nowhere to be seen. "Yeah. Just catching my breath," she said in between gasps of air. She hadn't run that fast in ages. She made a mental note to start her jogging routine the next day.

Georgia and Colt seemed to exchange a glance. He placed Georgia back on the ground and the dog immediately ran toward Bell. Showered in doggy kisses, Bell kneeled to be at the same height as her beloved canine.

"Oh, Georgia. I thought you were going to get hit. I was so worried." She rubbed Georgia's fuzzy ears as the dog soaked up the attention. Bell looked up, feeling highly aware that Colt was watching her. "So, you live here?"

The estate on which they stood in front was one of the prettiest on the street. All ivory marble and Corinthian columns. There was a giant willow tree in the front yard.

Colt smiled like they were old friends. "My family has had this house for generations. I came here every summer as a kid. It's... it's a pretty special place for me."

Bell nodded. "It's gorgeous. I can understand why you guys keep coming back. So does your family live here now?"

His face lit up. "My sister and my nieces are here now. My parents are doing an around-the-world trip. Dad had a heart attack last summer. They're trying to live each day like it's their last, or at least that's what they keep telling me every time I call. But they'll be here for the wedding. Maggie and I are just here to get the wedding stuff all straightened out." Colt's face became animated as he discussed his family. "But I'd love to move down here one day."

It was strange talking to Colt without Maggie. The tension in his jaw had eased and his shoulders were relaxed. He smiled. Bell hadn't seen him smile once in their meeting all together.

But then again, perhaps he simply hated wedding planning, she reminded herself.

Another squirrel came into view and Georgia instinctively went for it. This time, Bell had a proper grasp of the leash.

"She do that a lot?" Colt asked.

"Well, she's always a bit excitable," she began. "Okay maybe a bit more than I'd like. Especially for squirrels." Her heart was still thudding in her chest, and she drew Georgia nearer for a hug.

Colt shifted. "Have you taken her to dog training? Or those puppy classes? Whatever they're called?"

Bell shook her head. "Nah. She was an older girl when I got her. She's got some quirks, but I don't mind."

Colt continued. "Because my sister—the one I told you about. She trains dogs. She's really good."

Bell's interest piqued. "Oh yeah? Did she train your dog?"

Colt shook his head. "Nah. Don't have one. Maggie isn't much into animals."

Somehow that didn't surprise Bell. "Right." The breeze nipped at her cheeks. "Well, I'll consider it. I should get going. Georgia and I have had quite the day—"

"—Wait," Colt interrupted. He put his hands in his coat pockets, took them out again, and then put them back in. Bell realized that he looked *nervous*. "I want to apologize."

Bell's eyebrows shot up, and she re-adjusted Georgia's harness. "For what?"

Colt fidgeted with his gloves. "I know Maggie's been calling a lot. About wedding stuff. I want to, well, apologize. If it's a lot of work. I know... I know she's been giving you a bit of a hard time. She just wants the wedding to be perfect." He laughed nervously. "And I just want it to be perfect. For her."

Doing her best to hide her surprise, Bell shook her head. "No, no. It's been no problem at all. Of course, I'm going to do my best to make sure it's perfect," she said in her most convincing tone.

A wry smile formed on Colt's face. He didn't look like he bought it, but appeared grateful nonetheless. "Well, thanks."

Bell's phone beeped, signaling an incoming text message. Out of habit, she glanced at her phone in her open purse. The message was from Maggie.

Need to chat ASAP. Meet me at Wisteria????

She texted Maggie back straight away.

Hi Maggie, no problem. I'll be there in 30? Talk soon!

Bell drew a deep breath. "Speaking of, I'm due to meet your bride-to-be to discuss some wedding planning details now."

Colt frowned. "On a Saturday?"

Bell's eyes widened as she thought of a response. She didn't know why she was covering for Maggie. But she didn't want to let either of them down. "I'll occasionally work a weekend for special circumstances," she lied. She wasn't paid for overtime work, and her contract was standard working hours—except for weddings.

"Come on then. I'll give you a lift. If there's any more wedding planning that needs to be done, I might as well help," Colt offered.

"Oh, no. No that's not necessary," Bell insisted.

He shook his head. "Nonsense. I'm coming. Plus, I need to make sure Maggie doesn't want to add something that will spend us into debt for six lifetimes," he added with a grin.

Bell smiled uncertainly. Maggie had expensive taste. Their wedding was already clocking in at one of the most costly she had thrown.

Colt was already striding towards his Cameo truck in the driveway. Bell did her best to keep up. He fumbled with the keys before turning to her.

"You want to give it a go?" he said, handing her the keys.

Bell's eyes widened. She loved this truck. She also didn't want to wreck it. So far, she hadn't had much luck in the car department since arriving in Pink Shell Shores.

Colt seemed to hone in on her hesitation. "I should be more transparent. I actually fractured my right thumb the other day," he said, pulling off his glove to reveal a swollen and bruised right hand. "Trying to teach my niece how to play football," he said, shaking his head. "So I can't hold onto the gear shift all that well. You drive stick?"

Bell nodded, silently screaming in delight. The truck was beautiful. "Alright. But you have to hold onto Georgia."

Colt laughed. "Like that's a bad tradeoff. Come on Georgia," he said, reaching out to grab Georgia off the ground. "We're going to be best friends now."

Bell drove the two of them to the Wisteria Estate in record time—enjoying making good use of the Cameo's 145 horsepower, V8 engine. As she drove, she kept thinking they sure don't make 'em like they used to. Georgia stuck her head out of the open window, Colt clutching her protectively.

"Whoa there," Colt said. "I don't think anyone has ever driven that fast in Pink Shell Shores in the town's history. This is a sleepy place. No one's in a hurry."

She had gotten them there in less than ten minutes. Maggie's car was also in the parking lot. The dining room and bar at the Wisteria Estate remained open on weekends. Bell had a hunch that's where she would find Maggie.

"Yeah well, Pink Shell Shores just got their most recent Boston transplant. I'll take the slower pace of life and way fewer stores, but I can't quit all of my habits cold turkey. It might kill me," she joked.

Colt burst into laughter, lines forming around the corner of his eyes. Bell was a little taken aback. She had never seen him laugh like that.

"We're a little early," Bell said, checking her watch. "But I'm sure that won't matter." They were a whole twenty minutes early. Even though she worked there, Bell still felt taken aback whenever she walked into the Wisteria Estate. The opulence, the grandeur – it felt like from another time.

If that time period included copious amounts of pink.

Bell walked with Georgia tucked under one arm. She was certain that they had a 'no dogs allowed' policy, but Georgia was quiet and no one seemed to notice. They did a quick scan of the dining room before wandering into the bar. On weekends, the clientele was swankier. There was even a pianist playing at the white and gold baby grand piano. Waiters wore white jackets, and there was a hum of delighted chatter throughout the room.

"There she is," Colt said, brightening. He began waving toward Maggie, who was sitting at the bar. She didn't hear him. As they got closer, Terence came into view. He was chatting with Maggie.

A sinking feeling in her stomach began as Terence poured Maggie a drink. In a room full of people, they couldn't keep their eyes off of each other. They were glowing, hiding big smiles and sneaking glances at one another.

Even Colt seemed to notice, as a crease developed between his brows. Mid-laugh at something Terence said, Maggie turned. Her lighthearted eyes widened as she saw them, fear flashing across her face for an instant. Almost instantaneously, she composed herself.

"Colty!" Maggie sang. She got up off of her stool and walked, tripping slightly, over to them. "I didn't know you were coming too." Maggie shot daggers with her eyes towards Bell. A low grumbling sound came from Georgia.

Bell pretended not to notice.

"We're all here now," Bell said a little too casually as she pulled up a barstool for herself. "Hi Terence!" She smiled brightly at Terence.

Terence turned, taking in the three of them together. His jovial expression dropped before he recouped. "Bell! Nice to see you. Colt, my man," Terence said, reaching across the bar top to clap Colt on the shoulder. "What are we drinking?"

Bell glanced over at Colt. He was clenching and unclenching his jaw. "Scotch. Make it a double," Colt replied in even tones.

"Oh Colt. Lighten up. Be more adventurous, for once," Maggie pleaded. "Get a Wisteria Bubbly. That's what I've been drinking."

"I'll try that!" Bell added, trying to lighten the atmosphere. She took a seat, transferring Georgia to her purse. "Terence, I'll have one of those."

As Terence made their drinks, the three of them sat in silence. Colt and Maggie barely looked at each other.

"So, Maggie," Bell began, doing her best to inject enthusiasm into her voice. "What is it that needs wedding planning?"

Terence interrupted them. "Here you are, ladies. And Colt," he added, placing the drinks in front of them. Bell grabbed a glass of water, which she stealthily offered to Georgia.

Bell took a sip of her cocktail, resisting the urge to moan. Maggie had been right. It was *good*.

"So, shall we discuss wedding plans?" Bell tried again.

Maggie looked shifty eyed, taking another sip of her drink and hiccupping. Colt was staring into his drink. Bell had worked with couples that were fighting. But something was going on here.

Maggie's eyes lit up, her expression becoming animated. "You know what we should do?" Maggie paused dramatically, leaving Bell to wonder if she should throw out a few guesses. Bell wanted to suggest that they plan the wedding. Instead she smiled, doing her best to mirror Maggie's enthusiasm.

"Go over the order of events?" Bell offered, knowing that Maggie's mind had moved onto other things.

Maggie shook her head. "Wrong! Guess again."

"Plan the wedding?" She laughed, although it came out squeaky.

Maggie shook her head. "No. Something *fun*."

Colt looked up from his whiskey. "Maggie. Bell is our wedding planner. Maybe we should stick to that? Planning our wedding?"

Maggie laughed. A wounded look flashed across Colt's face, which he hid as he downed another sip. Maggie looked from Bell, to Colt, to Terence.

"Bell, I have got someone to set you up with. You're single, right?" Maggie asked.

Bell nearly spat out her drink. She must have heard that wrong. But Maggie was looking so pleased with herself. "What?" Bell breathed.

"With Terence!" Maggie said brightly. She seemed oblivious to Bell's discomfort.

Bell's cheeks were burning up. This could not be happening. She could feel all eyes on her. No way could she look up at Terence.

"How do you know she's single?" Colt offered.

Maggie sighed. "She doesn't have a ring on her finger. Plus, she was available today on such short notice," Maggie said, looking smug like she had solved a cold case.

It was official. Bell detested this woman. As she opened her mouth to protest, she was once again drowned out.

"A double date!" Maggie screamed in inspiration. "We absolutely must do a double date."

Georgia whined from the purse. Bell commiserated with her canine friend. She felt the same way.

Chapter Five

Bell didn't know if she had heard that correctly. Colt's expression was so baffled that Bell had to bite her lip to keep from laughing.

"A double date!" Maggie repeated herself, her eyes darting from Bell, to Colt, to Terence.

She had to be kidding, Bell couldn't help but think. But to her surprise and horror, Terence was already nodding.

"Shall I make reservations for the four of us? At La Valentin?" Terence asked casually.

How was this happening? Certainly, Colt would realize how weird it was. Bell snuck a glance in his direction. His deadpan expression gave nothing away.

"La Valentin? How romantic!" Maggie clasped her hands together. "Come on, Bell, you have to come. Remember? You said that you'd do anything to make my wedding perfect?"

Bell couldn't remember exactly saying those words. Even if she had, it hardly seemed appropriate to use them to wrangle her into a double date. Still, Harlow's words rang through her mind. *Everything. Must. Go. Smoothly.* Bell looked from Maggie, who pouted as she awaited confirmation. Terence looked like this whole situation was a game that he knew he was winning. She wasn't sure if she imagined Colt sitting up a little taller.

Morosely, Bell agreed. "Alright."

Maggie's face lit up. "Brilliant! I can't wait. Shall we say Sunday at seven? We can all meet there."

Colt checked his watch. "Great," he said tonelessly. "Now that that's settled, shall we get going? We're cutting it close for our dinner reservation," he said pointedly to Maggie, who seemed to take no notice.

"Bye dee bye!" Maggie trilled, giving a dainty wave of her fingers. Bell's stomach clenched and unclenched in relief as the pair of them left.

Bell was left at the bar across from Terence, whose interest in talking waned the moment that Maggie left. His reasons for agreeing to the double date were clearly *not* because of his interest in *her*. She downed her drink.

I may have to go on this date, Bell thought. *And when I do, I'm going to get to the bottom of this.* With that, she threw down a tip on the bar, told Terence she would see him tomorrow night, and left the Wisteria Estate. It was only as soon as she stepped outside that she remembered Colt had driven her. Desperate, she scanned the parking lot to see if she recognized anyone. She didn't. Letting out a wail in frustration, her eyes fixed on the pink vintage truck in the circular driveway. The 1930 Ford Model A Pickup. It made the Cameo ride earlier that day seem space age by comparison.

Sure, it was used for events and aesthetics. But it looked in working condition.

Harlow didn't work weekends. Terence's interest in her was spent. There was one more person she knew at the Wisteria Estate who might help...

"Mark!"

Within fifteen minutes, Mark from the front-desk had gotten clearance to provide Bell with a "temporary loan" for the car, provided she signed a few waivers that said she wouldn't sue the Wisteria Estate if driving the car resulted in injury to herself. She scribbled her initials on half a dozen places as Georgia barked in appreciation.

"You're a star!" Bell beamed at Mark, who flushed at the attention.

"I'm just glad you're getting home safe. I'd drive you myself, but my shift doesn't end for another few hours."

Bell smiled. "Well, chivalry suits you." She climbed up into the pink truck, feeling straight out of a movie. Mark had stepped out the door to make sure she knew how to put in into gear with the manual transmission. "I'll bring it back tomorrow," she called out the window as she expertly shifted from neutral to reverse. Everything inside felt new and shiny. It was hard to believe that anyone had ever owned the car, it was so well maintained.

"Don't bother," Mark leaned in and whispered. "I won't be in tomorrow. Going on a day trip outside of town. Monday works."

Bell beamed as she put the car into first gear, carefully driving out of the Wisteria Estate. This was a vehicle to be driven at a moderate pace with respect and reverence. She didn't know if it was all the talk about boyfriends, her upcoming date, or perhaps she was lonely, but she wished that Nigel could see her now.

Sunday night came much sooner than expected. Bell was seated next to Terence. Although it was plain that he was there for Maggie. They could barely keep their eyes off of each other.

Bell had done her best to be cordial. She had even spritzed on her favorite perfume, just in case she had been *way* off base and this *had* been a date.

It wasn't.

It turned out that her instincts had been spot on the first time. Colt had sat stone-faced the entire evening, his lasagna left untouched. He threw back another whiskey. Maggie tossed her head back, laughing at the punchline to one of Terence's jokes. Bell finished her glass of cabernet sauvignon, trying to get their waiter's attention that she would need another. *Soon.*

The entire evening, it seemed as though Bell and Colt were witnessing the budding of young love—between Maggie and Terence. The pair of them spoke as if they were the only ones there. At the beginning of the evening, Bell had tried to interject and steer the conversation towards more mutual topics. After Maggie kept redirecting the discussion back to Terence, Bell had given up. Colt seemed to be in his own world, observing Maggie as if an outsider. Bell didn't understand their relationship *at all.*

"Terence, tell the story of how you broke up that fight in the parking lot," Maggie enthused. Terence looked chuffed, opening his mouth to recount *yet* another story of his bravado.

"You know what? I think I'm just going to head on home," Colt said abruptly. "Bell, you mind giving Maggie a lift home? Since we're on the same street and all."

Bell was wide eyed in shock and nodded. "Sure. No problem."

Maggie pouted. "Colt. You're such a drama queen. Come on, sit down–"

"No, Maggie. I'm going. I'll see you at home," Colt said, shaking his head. He flagged down the waiter to pay.

As Colt walked away, Bell couldn't help but feel angry. What was Maggie's game? Was she trying to hurt him? Was she really that unkind?

Bell looked up to see Maggie and Terence exchanging a glance.

"I should get going too," Bell added, after Colt was gone. "Maggie, you want to come with me?"

Maggie looked at Terence and shook her head. "Nah. I'm going to give Colt some time to cool off. Terence can drive me home, right?"

Wide eyed, Bell did her best to hide her irritation. She muttered her goodbyes, furious as she left Le Valentin. If she had her suspicions before, she was certain now. Maggie was definitely in love. But it wasn't with Colt.

Chapter Six

That Monday started with a mountain of paperwork. Bell had to meet with Juniper, a florist who promised that she could get as many pink orchids as Bell needed. It would come at a price. Bell was dubious, but Juniper was her last shot. No one else near Pink Shell Shores had pink orchids. She breathed a sigh of relief after checking her voice messages, the meeting later that afternoon confirmed. A knock came from Bell's office door.

"Come in!"

Bell expected it to be Harlow. Perhaps Maggie. She certainly hadn't expected it to be Colt. Standing there, looking relatively shame-faced, he uncertainly took a few steps into her office.

"Hey there." he said, his eyes not meeting hers. "I—uh—I wanted to apologize for last night."

Bell shook her head. This was unbelievable. Maggie acted the way she did, and Colt was the one apologizing? "Seriously, you don't have to apologize," she said earnestly. Thinking back to yesterday's evening plans made her fume.

Colt looked uncomfortable, his eyes darting around her office. "You mind if I sit?" he asked, motioning to the empty seat in front of her.

"No, no, not at all. Take a seat," she offered.

Colt ran his hand through his hair, his jaw clenched. What was going on? His gaze finally settled on hers.

"I'll just come out and ask," he said, as if forcing himself. "You work with a lot of couples, right?"

Bell nodded. "Hundreds through the years. Why do you ask?"

Colt fidgeted with his watch before taking a deep breath. "Do you feel like you know which couples are going to make it or not? Like, did you have a sixth sense beforehand when a wedding was called off?"

Bell was stunned. Was Colt telling her that the wedding was off? Just because of last night? She wanted to tell him: "Yes!" She typically had a feeling about couples. It certainly didn't take an expert to see that he and Maggie were struggling.

"I think Maggie wants to call off the wedding," Colt whispered, his eyes fixed on the floor.

Bell gaped at Colt. Here was this sweet, kind man, besotted by his fiancé who was treating him terribly. She wanted to tell him: "You'll be better off! She doesn't deserve you!" Of course, she said no such thing.

Treading lightly, Bell prodded. "What makes you say that?"

Colt laughed bitterly, his eyes meeting hers. "You were at the dinner last night. I don't think I have to spell it out."

A cold feeling ran through her as she felt Colt's pain. She had been in his shoes. Rapid-fire memories came back to her when she had found out that Nigel was sleeping with that girl from reception. She winced at the recollection.

"So, so you think she wants to be with Terence?" she found herself asking.

Colt shook his head, as if he could hardly believe it. "I don't know. I mean, it's *Maggie*," he said, as if that explained it all. When Bell didn't respond, he continued. "She's always been flirty. That's just how she is. I know that. But she never crosses the line. *Never*," he said with resolve, like he was trying to convince himself. "This time. I don't know. Something feels different."

Bell pulled a face. "I'll admit, there seems like there's been some tension between the two of you."

Colt nodded. "So it's not just me? You see it too?"

Bell felt acutely aware of her role. She was their wedding planner. Maggie was as much her client as Colt. But, the pain in Colt's eyes felt all too real. She had been there. She had sat in his position. When she had those inkling suspicions that Nigel was cheating on her, it hadn't been an easy thing to stomach.

"Have you spoken to Maggie?" Bell asked. She wondered what Maggie thought of all of this.

Colt sighed, like he had this discussion before. "She won't answer me directly. Whenever I bring it up, she leaves. I haven't been able to reach her all morning. I don't know if I'm being paranoid... I want to be trusting. But, since you're an expert in this, I just wanted to see... you know... your thoughts." Colt looked like he had run out of steam.

Bell took a deep breath. She commiserated with his pain. "Look, I don't know what I can do to help," Bell began. "But if you think of anything, just let me know."

Colt nodded, the crease between his brows smoothing. "Thanks." He stood to his feet, looking shy as he smiled. "Just, let me know if you hear anything?"

Bell smiled as optimistically as she could. "Will do."

As Colt left, her heart ached for him. Not just because she had been through it all before. But because Bell knew that her feelings for him were growing by the second.

Twelve o'clock struck and Bell wandered into Tea Readings. She needed a break. As soon as she saw Chantal at the counter, Bell broke into a smile.

"Hi Chantal!" Bell greeted her. Bell had always paid close attention to names. She never forgot them. She found most people weren't the same, often forgetting her name on the second meeting. She was often met with: "Oh, yes. Um, hi!" or even once "Ball, was it?"

Bell was pleasantly surprised as Chantal turned to her, recognition dawning on her face. "Bell! Where's your friend Georgia today?"

Bell beamed. She knew she had liked Chantal right off the bat. Now it was cemented. "She's at home. I wish I could bring her in to work," she mused aloud. "Maybe one day. Is Penny in today?"

"Not today. She's with the girls." Chantal pointed to a picture of the pair of them and two young girls.

"Your daughters?" Bell ventured, and Chantal beamed.

"How's work going? You liking the Wisteria Estate?" Chantal asked.

Bell smiled. "It's incredible. Such a beautiful venue."

Chantal nodded. "You must be planning the Gamay wedding? That's coming up quick."

"Does everyone know everyone in this town?" she asked.

Chantal smiled. "Oh, *everyone* knows. I got to meet his future bride the other day now that they're back in Pink Shell

Shores. Not the kind of woman I would have expected Colt to be with."

"Oh yeah?"

Chantal frowned. "I shouldn't have said anything. Now, what can I get you?" Chantal asked, returning to her jovial demeanor.

"A red-eye, please and thanks," Bell said, stifling a yawn. "I'm going to need it for the rest of the day."

The following weeks flew by. Bell's time was occupied with vendor appointments, calls to re-confirm the caterers and the engravers, searching for hairstylists and makeup artists who met Maggie's near impossible standards, a seemingly never ending trail of text messages from Maggie... and Bell still couldn't find those swans. The pressure was building, especially with the Valentine's Day wedding now seven days away. The one thing that seemed to go well was meeting with the florist, Jupiter, who promised that she would have all the pink orchids the day of the wedding. She had to admit that the sample bouquets provided were stunning. Bell had texted Maggie a photo of them and had gotten approval to go ahead.

"I'm going to have to tell her," Bell complained to Harlow, who was penciling in her eyebrows at her desk.

"She's going to have to deal. You've gone above and beyond. Plus, there's nothing you can do. It's a service that doesn't exist," Harlow sighed, snapping shut her compact mirror. "I don't like it, but sometimes our brides can't get exactly what they dreamed of."

Bell's whole body relaxed as soon as she heard those words escape Harlow's mouth. It was enough to disappoint Maggie, but to disappoint Harlow too? It would have been too much.

She hadn't even admitted to Harlow about the escalating tension between Colt and Maggie. Whenever Harlow asked how things were going, Bell would underplay it, her fingers crossed behind her back.

"Thank you," Bell breathed. "Now, I'm meeting Maggie in the gardens in ten."

Harlow's eyebrows raised. "The gardens? But it's February."

Bell shrugged. "Who knows? Apparently she wants to check out the lighting for the photos. I'll break the news to her about the swans then."

"Make sure you follow it with some good news," Harlow cautioned. "We want everything to go smoothly... or in this case, at least as smoothly as possible," she added as an afterthought.

Bell nodded, licking her chapped lips. "Right. No problem at all."

She headed to the gardens, which even in the wintertime were stunning. She was a little early—a habit of hers. It seemed that Maggie was too. Maggie stood on the wisteria-covered bridge. She wasn't alone.

She opened her mouth to call out Maggie's name when she saw his face. Her heart sank, and breathlessly, Bell stood watching them. It was just as she expected. Terence gave Maggie a quick peck on the lips as he slid away, leaving Maggie alone. She was shocked. Of course, Bell had her suspicions. But she had never once caught a bride in the act. Frozen, Bell was prepared to leave when Maggie saw her and locked eyes. A flash of fear crossed Maggie's face as she drew her hand to her lips.

There was nothing in Bell's education that had taught her how to handle such a delicate situation. Even her past experience was no match for this. She was at a loss. Maggie walked over to her slowly, Bell's mind still reeling.

Maggie spoke first, her head held high. "Bell, we need to talk."

Chapter Seven

Bell must have heard incorrectly. She shook her head as Maggie repeated herself yet again.

"You *can't* tell Colt," Maggie insisted. To Maggie's credit, she *did* look remorseful, her eyes welling with tears.

"So you're telling me that you're in love with Terence *and* Colt?" Bell echoed.

Nodding, Maggie fiddled with her engagement ring. "I–I always thought I would marry Colt. We were happy. Sort of. I mean, we fought a lot. Especially about the wedding. When I met Terence, everything with him felt easy."

Indignation was bubbling in Bell, who took steady breaths to manage her temper. "So what do you want me to do?" she said finally.

"Nothing," Maggie replied immediately.

"Nothing?" Bell echoed. There was no way Maggie could be serious. But Maggie nodded her head.

"I gave Colt my word," Maggie said, as if *now* her morals were kept to the highest standard. "I couldn't betray him."

Bell wanted to tell Maggie that she had already betrayed him, but she shook her head instead. Harlow's words echoed in her head. *Everything must go smoothly.*

Maggie continued. "That's why I wanted to meet you with last Saturday at the Wisteria. I wanted to ask you your opinion."

Bell gawked. "My opinion on what? You having a pre-wedding fling?"

Maggie looked stricken. "No, I mean, I don't know..."

Bell couldn't look Maggie in the eye, she was beyond upset. If there was ever a time for some tough love, Bell knew that it was now. "You can't get the swans you want. It's a service that doesn't exist," Bell said bluntly. "And the engravers can do a rush job, but it will cost extra."

Maggie frowned but said nothing. Nodding slowly, Bell realized that Maggie was close to tears. "Okay," Maggie said.

Her tears didn't elicit any feelings of sympathy from Bell. "Good. Now, I've got a few other things to catch up on. Until then, I think the wedding is mostly covered. All I need from you at this point is to show up to our scheduled appointments. We can review it all a few days before. Sounds good?" Bell said in stilted tones.

Maggie nodded, her eyes fixed on the ground.

"Good. I'll see you soon." Bell turned on her heel, feeling the need to scream. Somehow, she held it together as she walked into Harlow's office and shut the door.

"What's wrong?" Harlow asked, looking up from her computer.

Bell took a series of deep breaths. "I know that it's important to make sure everything goes smoothly. But, um..."

"What? It's probably not as bad as you think," Harlow said, her eyes widening.

"I just saw Maggie kissing someone outside. And it wasn't Colt," Bell blurted before she could stop herself.

Harlow's eyes widened. "No!"

"Yes!"

Harlow slowly shook her head. "Well, can't say I've seen this before. Also, who was she kissing?"

Bell shifted. She didn't want to rat out Terence. She avoided Harlow's stern gaze.

"Don't tell me. Terence?" Harlow asked in a knowing tone. Bell's expression seemed to give it away and Harlow shook her head. "He's always been flirty with brides. We've had to warn him in the past. But never *this*."

"I don't want to get him in trouble," Bell said, nerves overcoming her. "I mean, maybe he's in love with her," she mused.

Harlow didn't look sold. "I guess that's one wedding you don't have to keep planning."

Bell snapped into focus. "No. No, no. She still wants to marry Colt."

Harlow threw her head back and laughed. "Now I've heard everything. That girl wants to have two cakes and eat them both at the same time."

"So should I tell Colt?"

Harlow stiffened. "I wish it was that simple," Harlow began. She looked at Bell with fondness. "Look, our job as wedding planners at the Wisteria is to give people their dream wedding. It might not be *our* dream wedding, but we have to be able to get through the bumps. Sometimes, our job means being discreet. To help smooth rough patches."

Bell felt her heart sink into her stomach. "Right."

"But," Harlow added. "If he were to find out on his own, there would be nothing you could do in that case."

Harlow peered at Bell with thickly mascaraed lashes and winked.

Chapter Eight

Sipping her hot chocolate with Georgia curled up in her lap, Bell was up past her bedtime and going over the wedding itinerary once again. Maggie and Colt's wedding was five days away. Bell had five days to try to help Colt understand what he was getting himself into. If he hadn't already confessed his suspicions to her, there would have been a chance that Bell would have stayed out of it. She would have thought: maybe they were into that sort of stuff? She had heard of stranger things.

But Bell knew. Colt would be devastated. Scratch that—his marriage would be a sham. He would be devoted to Maggie, and Maggie would be devoted to Terence. It didn't seem like an ideal scenario.

If Bell had been in Colt's shoes, she would want someone to run up to her and tell her right away. If she didn't believe it, she would want them to shout it to her until she did. She wasn't in Colt's shoes. She was their wedding planner. She had to tread carefully. There were always two sides to every story. Bell didn't even know the *one* side fully.

Since she had caught Maggie and Terence, Maggie had been *extra* nice to Bell. Maggie had laid off the demanding text messages. It was an unexpected relief not to wake up to five new requests the last two mornings. Maggie had even brought Bell a gift basket and left it at reception, with an uber-sweet note thanking her for her hard work and a bunch of bath products.

"She's trying to pay you off," Lacey said over the phone in response to Bell's late night plea for help from her twin sister. One thing between them remained constant over the years—it was never too late to call.

"You think?" Bell asked, taking a thoughtful sip of hot chocolate. Georgia was snoring and asleep on her foot.

"It's hush money. Or in her case, hush bubble-bath." Bell couldn't help but laugh as Lacey continued. "Wake up and smell the evil bride!" Lacey cried. "Tell me you're going to tell the groom."

Bell paused. She didn't want to lie to her sister, but she didn't want to tell her the truth either. "So how's everything in Boston?" she tried to change the subject.

"Nah uh. You're not getting off that easy. You have to tell him, Bell. It's not right."

Bell sighed. Easy for Lacey to say. "You think it's terrible if I don't tell him?" Bell asked. A huge part of her wanted to chicken out. Confrontation had never been her strong suit.

"If you don't, I think you'll really regret it. Besides, it would be so much harder to tell him after they're married. And it's not like she's going to stop. If she's cheating now, she'll do it later too."

Bell didn't want to argue with her sister about the probability and likeliness that Maggie would continue cheating on Colt. Once Lacey's mind was made up, that was that. There was no changing it. Bell believed that people *could* change. Georgia whined from Bell's foot and meandered towards the door, looking outside with baleful eyes.

"I should get going," Bell said, grabbing Georgia's harness. "Georgia hasn't had her final walk."

"Okay. But before you go, I wanted to tell you our big news." Lacey gave a dramatic paused before blurting it out. "We're coming to visit you!"

Bell's mouth dropped open. "That's incredible! When?"

"Probably a few weeks? I'll let you know soon. Gunner has to finalize a few things."

Bell perked up. She felt extra-grateful for some good news. "Well, come anytime. I cannot wait to show you Pink Shell Shores and the Wisteria!"

"Unches and bunches and funches!" they said to each other before ringing off.

Bell had gotten halfway down Oyster Lane when she heard the shouting.

"...you don't understand... big mistake..." It sounded like Maggie's voice.

Bell walked up to the stately home that Colt's family owned. On the lawn stood Colt and Maggie having a one-sided screaming match, with Maggie doing all the yelling.

"It didn't mean anything!" she wailed as Colt put bags into his truck. A pang of tightness hit Bell right in the chest.

He knows.

Feeling paralyzed with curiosity, her fear of being seen got the better of her. She continued on her way with Georgia.

"What are you going to do? You know I'm sorry. I said that. What more do you want?" Maggie continued to whine, seeming more frantic by the second.

It was Maggie's high-pitched voice that piqued Georgia's attention. As Georgia saw Colt, she made a bolt for it. This time, Bell held tightly to her leash. It didn't stop Georgia from barking and attracting unwanted attention.

Both Colt and Maggie's heads swiveled toward Georgia, who was doing her best to run toward Colt. Too caught off guard to speak, Bell held up her hand and waved good-naturedly. Maybe they would think she hadn't heard them.

Colt stopped loading the truck and faced her. "Bell, so sorry. Shouldn't be making so much noise so late at night. But good. I'm glad to run into you. Cancel the wedding plans." Although he spoke calmly, Bell observed the rigidity of his jaw. His quick, short movements. His nervous, darting glances. He wouldn't make eye contact with anyone but Georgia. Appearing purposeful, he strode forward and bent down to give Georgia's little head a rub.

Bell's heart sunk to her stomach. He was serious. She could see it in his eyes. The hurt. The betrayal. The confusion, doubt, and anger. She had been there. She wished she could trade places with him, taking away his hurt.

Maggie's eyes widened as she grabbed his shoulders. "You can't be serious, Colty," she pleaded. "You can't cancel the wedding. Not for this..." she sputtered.

Colt shook his head in disbelief as he turned toward Bell. "Cancel the plans. All of them," he said to Bell. Turning to Maggie, hurts flashing in his eyes. Opening his mouth to speak, he paused before closing it. He turned on his heel, stepping into the Chevy Cameo and shutting the door with a thud. With the rev of his engine, Colt Gamay was gone, leaving behind a single and seriously pissed off Maggie.

Maggie turned to Bell, her eyes now blazing with fury. "You're our wedding planner. Fix this!"

Early the next morning, Bell had called an emergency meeting with Harlow, who met her at the Wisteria Estate. After they were alone in Harlow's office, Bell told Harlow the full story.

Harlow exhaled dramatically. "There's *nothing* worse than a cheater."

Bell nodded, wondering if Harlow was speaking from experience. "I hope Colt is all right."

"Oh, he'll be fine," Harlow said with a wave of her hand. "We've all been there."

Her eyebrows shot up. "Oh yeah?" She didn't want to press Harlow on it. Despite everything, Harlow was still her boss.

Harlow nodded. "Oh yeah. My husband—*ex*-husband, I should say—found another woman. Right after I had just had my first daughter," she laughed. "I felt awful about myself at the time. I had gained a bunch of weight during my pregnancy, didn't feel like myself anymore, my body felt totally different..."

Bell's eyes were like saucers as she listened. She couldn't imagine Harlow feeling self-conscious. Not in a million years. Whenever Bell had talked to her, Harlow hadn't seemed to have a shred of self-doubt. Harlow was just so... *Harlow*. In her tight red dress with her even redder hair tied in a trendy bun on top of her head, she was the postcard picture of glamor.

Harlow continued. "So, like I say. There is *nothing* worse than a cheater. Not even a spoiled wedding."

Harlow spoke with such repugnancy. All that Bell could do was nod. She agreed. Yet at the same time, she couldn't shake that image of Colt's expression when he left.

"I felt like something was up the second I met Maggie," Harlow continued. Bell smiled wanly. She had too. For Colt's sake, Bell wished that she had been totally, one hundred per-cent, *completely* wrong about Maggie.

Chapter Nine

A full day had passed since watching the fallout between Colt and Maggie. She had barely heard a word from either of them since. She had called both of them to confirm that canceling the wedding was really what they wanted. Maggie hadn't answered her phone or her text messages. Colt had sent a single word text message back—yes. At Harlow's urging, Bell had been busy all day calling the vendors and canceling. After all, it was what Colt had said he wanted.

It wasn't a fun job.

With her shoulders heavy and a twinge of a headache that was threatening to worsen, Bell left the Wisteria Estate. She felt ready for a glass of wine at home in front of the fire with Georgia beside her. All day, she had been plagued with thoughts of Colt. How was he doing? Bell couldn't imagine anyone choosing Terence over Colt. She couldn't think of choosing *anyone* over Colt. Not that she had that choice, she reminded herself.

As Bell drove onto Oyster Lane, she saw an unfamiliar SUV pull up into her driveway. Her mind immediately went to Colt, but that was silly since it wasn't his truck. She turned into her driveway and parked behind the vehicle, noticing the Massachusetts's license plate.

The two passenger doors of the SUV burst open and two pint-sized people jumped out and ran towards her car. "Aunty Bell!"

It was Presley and Olivia running towards her with rosy cheeks and big smiles. Grinning, Bell climbed out of the Superbeetle and gave her two nieces a big hug. Lacey and Gunner stood with equally big grins behind them and a bottle of red wine in hand.

"What are you guys doing here?" Bell breathed, happily accepting the kisses her nieces were planted on her cheeks.

"Mom said we were doing a big surprise." Olivia said matter-of-factly.

"Surprise!" yelled Presley.

Misty eyed, Bell blinked back tears. She hadn't realized just how much she missed her family. Presley was missing a tooth, and Olivia seemed to be even taller than she remembered. Lacey looked the same in her shearling coat and Gunner, behind his smile, had the distinct look exhaustion with dark circles under his eyes. Bell gave them each a huge hug as Gunner grabbed the bags from their SUV.

"When did you guys get here?" Bell asked breathlessly.

"We got to town an hour ago. We've been exploring town. We *love* Pink Shell Shores," Lacey said emphatically.

Bell felt like she was in her own dream as they walked up to her front door. As she opened her peach-colored door, Lacey gasped. "It's gorgeous!"

Presley and Olivia ran inside, and Georgia began barking and jumping in all the excitement.

"Nice place," Gunner said, looking around admiringly. "You find it hard to get a place out here in the winter?" he asked, looking genuinely curious. Lacey and Gunner looked at her expectantly.

"Don't tell me you guys are interested?" Bell asked, her eyes widening and her smile growing by the second.

Lacey beamed. "You never know..."

As Bell gave them a tour of her new place, she couldn't help but feel a burst of pride. "This is it!"

Lacey and Gunner *oohed* and *aahed* over the ocean in her backyard, the fireplace, the light. "Seems like everything here is going really well for you," Gunner said.

Bell felt herself turning pink. "Thanks, Gunner. I guess things are going well." It wasn't usual that Gunner offered such words of praise. He was usually doling out advice or smart remarks. Lacey was looking at everything from top to bottom. Were they just excited for her? Or was there something more?

Georgia stopped running around, walked over to her leash and turned to look up at them. "I think it's time for me to take her out," Bell said, before Gunner interjected.

"No, no. I can do it. Give you and Lace some time to catch up," he said. "If that's alright," he quickly added.

Bell smiled. "Yeah, that's great. Thanks Gunner." Presley and Olivia shouted that they wanted to come too, running through the door like lightning.

As soon as they were alone, Bell's attention snapped to her sister. "What's going on?"

Lacey feigned shock. "What ever are you talking about?" she asked, bringing her hand to her chest.

"Come on. You guys show up out of the blue, super interested in Pink Shell Shores, Gunner looks exhausted and even he seemed into it—"

Lacey's face crumpled. "Oh, Bell. The last few months have been, well, *rough*."

"Rough?" Bell echoed. "But I thought Gunner just got that promotion?"

Lacey nodded. "He did. Things were already strained between Gunner and I. I mean, his entire life was all about work. And when he got that promotion, it was nuts. He was stressed all the time. Then last week..." She drew her finger along her neck. "...they fired him."

"*Fired* him?"

"Yeah. It really shook his self-esteem," Lacey said thoughtfully. "On the plus side, we've gotten the chance to re-evaluate what we want."

Bell frowned. All this time, Lacey had been keeping this from her. But then she thought back to their last few phone conversations. It had been all about her. Her move. Her big adventures. A pang of guilt hit her. "So, what do you think you want?" She bit her lip, awaiting a response.

Lacey's face lit up. "I want to work. And Gunner's going to stay home with the kids."

Bell thought back to Lacey's job before she had Olivia and Presley. Lacey had worked as a manager of three Italian restaurants in downtown Boston. Those had been long hours that Lacey worked. "You want to go back to the restaurant business?"

Lacey laughed. "No. Nothing like that. Maybe I'll go back to school. Take some classes. Maybe we'll move down here!" she explained. "I've always wanted to teach, you know. Maybe work with kids. Or perhaps something related to art..."

Their conversation was cut short as Georgia, Gunner, Presley, and Olivia barreled through the doors. Bell looked closely at Gunner—it was clear. He looked exhausted. But he looked happy. Bell turned to her sister, who was gazing at them with adoration.

This whole time, Bell had thought Lacey's life was perfect. Without so much as a ripple in the fabric. Now, as Bell watched Gunner play fighting with Georgia, Olivia running in circles with one shoe, and Presley now perched beside her loudly repeating that she was "braiding her hair", Bell realized that Lacey's life was so much more than perfect. It was *real*.

The next few days, with no particular wedding deadline looming, passed uneventfully. Bell drove past Colt's family house on Oyster Lane. Each time, she craned her neck to see if his truck was parked in the driveway. It never was. At the Wisteria Estate, Bell had been briefed on her new couples and their upcoming weddings. There was a conference she had to schedule within the month. Things were going like clockwork. Not even a whisper of a bridezilla in sight.

So on Valentine's Day, when Bell received a knock on her door, she was shocked to see that it was Colt. She could barely keep her jaw from dropping.

"How are you?" he asked, a nervous smile plastered on his face. He looked like a different man. Standing tall, there was a glint in his eye. That stubborn crease between his brows had smoothed.

"I'm—I'm doing fine," she stammered. Just the sight of him gave her butterflies. Her cheeks already felt flushed. "The better question is, how are you?"

Colt put his hands in his coat pockets. "I've been good, actually. Really good, in fact."

Bell took him in. Was this the same man who had found out his fiancé was cheating on him just a few days earlier? More importantly, why was he here?

Colt seemed to read her mind. His eyes fixed on hers, Bell's stomach flip-flopped. "I know it's weird that I'm here. But, I was wondering if I could ask you something. Maybe we could take Georgia for a walk?"

"Aunty Bell! Who is this?" Presley and Olivia came barreling down the stairs. The two of them stood in their pajamas, staring up at Colt.

He looked from her nieces back to Bell. "Are these your daughters?" he asked with a grin.

Bell shook her head. "Nieces. They're my twin sister's kids."

"Speaking of your twin sister," Lacey said, popping up from behind Colt as she stepped inside after a brisk run. Unlike Bell, Lacey was an avid jogger. She extended her hand. "Hi, I'm Lacey."

"It's nice to meet you all," Colt said, looking from face to face. He looked like he genuinely meant it, to Bell's relief.

"Are you married?" Presley asked him, blinking at him with those big round eyes of hers.

Bell felt herself reddening from the tips of her fingers to her cheeks. "She's just kidding," Bell said. Georgia ran over and began yelping at her feet.

Colt laughed. "No, no, I'm not married," he said to Presley, who seemed to be digesting this information.

"Mommy and daddy are going to get married again!" Olivia said, throwing her hands in the air.

Lacey rolled her eyes good-naturedly. "The girls want my husband and I to renew our vows. Do the whole thing over again," she explained to Colt, who nodded upon hearing this. It was true. Since arriving in Pink Shell Shores, Lacey and Gunner had been mulling over a myriad of new ideas. Including matching tattoos, which was quickly nixed.

"Well, I can understand that. Weddings are a lot of fun," he said to Lacey and Olivia. "A lot of work," he added to Lacey and Bell.

"And a lot of time, which I don't have!" Lacey said, throwing her head back to laugh. Lacey eyed Bell very *un*subtly, and clapped her hands together. "Okay girls. Let's go get some lunch put together. Who likes macaroni?"

"Me!" shouted Presley.

"I do!" said Olivia.

Lacey said her goodbye to Colt and with a wink to Bell, set off to the kitchen—two very excited children in tow.

Colt beamed at Bell. "So, about that walk?"

Bell nodded, doing her best to keep her excitement under wraps. As she took Georgia's harness and got her ready, she was distracted by an incoming phone call which she ignored. Nothing felt as important as this moment. As she fastened Georgia's harness, Bell's phone rang again. And again. She peered at the phone number. It looked familiar, but she couldn't place it.

Telling Colt she would just be a minute, Bell answered. "Hello?"

"Bell!" came the voice on the other end. "It's Jupiter. I've been trying to reach you for ages now. I've got all the pink orchids here for the Gamay-Blazer wedding. Where do you want 'em?"

Chapter Ten

B ell was speechless.

"Hello?" Jupiter asked. "You still there?"

Swallowing hard, Bell nodded—realizing that Jupiter couldn't hear that. "Yes," she said. "I'm still here."

"So where do you want me to put flowers?"

Bell could just imagine them. Tens of thousands that Maggie had insisted on spending to ensure that the floral displays at the wedding would instill awe in every guest.

"But, but we canceled the flowers," she said.

"That's true," Jupiter countered. "But Ms. Blazer called to tell us the wedding was back on. There's a wedding happening today, from what I understand."

Bell peered at Colt. He was clean-shaven today. His hair was neatly combed. He *could* pass as someone getting married that day.

"I'll be there in ten minutes," she found herself saying.

As Colt played with Georgia, Bell immediately rang Maggie. She hadn't spoken to Maggie since that incident several days ago. Maggie hadn't answered her phone until this point and now answered on the first ring.

"Bell!" Maggie trilled. "I'm so glad you called. I'm at the Wisteria now. Everything looks like it's going great."

Bell was too shocked to say anything. Had she missed something? Had she developed dementia? Or early onset

Alzheimer's? Gripped in fear at the thought, she looked at her phone for confirmation. Still February fourteenth. She took a deep breath.

"Maggie, what are you talking about? The wedding was canceled."

"That's what you think. And Colt thinks. But just you wait," Maggie said, the line going dead. Bell stared from her phone to Colt.

"Colt," Bell began, her voice hoarse. "Just got a bit of a weird call..." Then she yelled into the kitchen. "Lace, I've got to go out for a while. Be back soon."

Colt drove Bell to the estate. He kept muttering under his breath, "She can't be serious." Bell sat in stunned silence. She thought she had seen it all. Clearly not.

The pair of them pulled up to the Wisteria Estate. From outside the front entrance, Mark looked frazzled, gesturing wildly at someone carrying a sleuth of pink bouquets. He looked relieved to see her as she ran up to see what was happening.

"Bell!" Mark yelled, his eyes wide and frantic. "I don't know what's happening. The flowers. They won't stop."

Bell peered through the open door, her jaw all but hitting the floor. "What—what is all this?" she stammered. The lobby of the Wisteria Estate was packed full of pink orchids. She had to admit, it looked stunning.

"I can answer that," came a voice. Bell's head swiveled to see Maggie walking down the staircase. If she had felt shocked before, it was nothing compared to seeing Maggie in a wedding dress. She turned to Colt—apparently she wasn't alone in feeling shocked. Colt's eyes were wide, a bewildered expression on his face. That didn't seem to deter Maggie as she sidled up to him.

"I've missed you, Colty," Maggie said, taking his hands in hers. "Let's get married."

Colt screwed up his face, pulling his hands away. "Are you insane?" he sputtered. Maggie looked wounded before she tried another angle. "I did all of this, for us," she said, twirling around.

They were surrounded by pink orchids, and out of the corner of her eye, Bell noticed a photographer taking test shots outside. Were those wedding guests pulling up in the parking lot?

Colt shook his head. "No, Maggie."

"But Colt—"

"—I've had enough!" he exploded, making even Maggie take a step back. "I've had it with your behavior. You've treated me terribly. I've had the past week to think about it. You completely take me for granted... And now this! This is totally just... unbelievable!"

Bell's pulse quickened. She wanted to tell Colt, "Way to go!" but instead watched in a stupor.

"...you are a bully, Maggie. Plain and simple," Colt said.

Maggie's expression soured. Pursing her lips, she turned to Bell. "Is it because of *her*?" she asked accusingly.

Bell wished she didn't have a front-row seat. Colt shook his head. "Maggie, we're over. Remember? Over. Done. You cheated on me and then refused to take no for an answer. You don't listen to me."

"But Colt—" Maggie began before stopping herself. Looking down, she nodded as if hearing him for the first time. "Alright," she said, after what felt like an eternity of silence.

Bell stepped away as covertly as possible, giving the former-couple some space. She felt misty-eyed herself, hearing it all. Mark looked like he had seen a ghost, as Bell ushered him outside.

"I don't understand," he fumbled. "Was there a wedding scheduled that I missed? I swear, I looked at the schedule twice, and Harlow never mentioned it..."

Bell patted him on the shoulder. "No, Mark. You didn't miss a thing."

A woman Bell recognized as Juniper sauntered over with another display of pink orchids. Bell sighed. They really were beautiful. "Where do you want me to put these?" Juniper asked.

"Wherever you like," Bell heard from behind her. Colt was walking up, a look of mutual sadness and relief on his face. He turned to face Bell. "I think there's someone here who could totally use a wedding today."

Colt began to smile, and it dawned on Bell.

"Why yes, I think you're right. I think today is the *perfect* day for a wedding." She whipped out her phone and began to send Lacey a text message. Mid-way through typing, she glanced at Colt. "Just to clarify, you meant Lacey and Gunner, right?"

Colt grinned. "If they're into pink orchids, then this could be their lucky day."

Chapter Eleven

Bell held onto Olivia and Presley's hands as they tossed petals into the air. Lacey and Gunner looked radiant. In a lace shawl and cream-colored sweater dress, Lacey looked every bit a bride with her ear-to-ear smile. Jupiter had even fussed with Lacey's hair, so she had pink orchids cascading through her hair. Gunner even looked like his former self—smiling and pleased to see Lacey so happy. The pair had seemed dubious at first, wondering if it was a joke or not. But as Bell explained, it was exactly what they wanted. "A quiet, intimate, family-oriented ceremony," Bell had said. "Isn't that what you wanted, Lacey?"

Lacey beamed as she kissed Gunner and beneath an archway of pink wisteria and orchids in the garden of the Wisteria Estate. All the staff members at the Wisteria Estate had come out to watch, their eyes becoming misty. Colt had even called his sister and two nieces, Layla and Sandrine, who were watching from the sidelines.

"Yay! Mummy and daddy married!" Olivia screamed.

"Married!" echoed Presley. The two of them in their fluffy dresses looked like the perfect bridesmaids.

Lacey walked by, tears gleaming in her eyes. "Thank you," she mouthed to Bell, as Gunner swooped her up for a spin. The crowd whooped and cheered.

As someone began handing out glasses of champagne, Presley and Olivia ran off to play with Colt's nieces.

Colt began walking up to her, with a familiar face in tow.

"Penny!" Bell smiled. "So nice to see you again."

Penny gave Bell a big hug. "Thank you so much for taking such good care of my brother, here," she said, poking Colt in the shoulder. Bell looked from Penny to Colt, the resemblances between them becoming clearer. "I always told Chantal I didn't see it, him and Maggie," Penny added.

Colt cleared his throat. "Yes, well..."

"Sorry," Penny added, pulling a face. She looked from Colt to Bell and smiled. "I'll leave you two be. I should get back. Chantal is minding Tea Readings while I'm here. I should pop back. Layla. Sandrine. Let's go! Remind me," she called to Bell as she walked away, her daughters in tow. "I still have to do your reading!"

Bell smiled. "Don't worry, I'll be in soon!"

Mark and Harlow, both in attendance, began ushering people inside where the pianist was playing. The entire dining room at the Wisteria Estate had been decorated for Valentine's Day. In addition to pink orchids, there were even more flowers. *Everywhere.* Lacey looked beside herself in happiness, and Bell watched as Lacey, Gunner, Presley, and Olivia walked into the Wisteria Estate all holding hands.

It was quite something.

"Thank you," Bell whispered to Colt. "Thank you so much. You made them so happy."

Colt shrugged, a bashful smile forming on his face. "Might as well put all of this to good use," he said, exhaling hard. "I actually came to your house this morning to ask you something."

Bell's heart thudded in her chest. "You mean you didn't come over to ask if my sister wanted to have a big wedding, which was supposed to be yours?"

Colt shook his head. "Nah. I wanted to see if you wanted to grab dinner. It is Valentine's Day, after all."

Chapter Twelve

Two Months Later

April in Pink Shell Shores was even more beautiful than Bell had expected. The Wisteria Estate was at its peak, as far as she was concerned. "Just wait until the summer," was all that Harlow continued to say with a smirk. The wisteria vines were blossoming everywhere. Often, Bell's mind flashed to Colt. She wondered where he was. What he was doing. They had gone for an enjoyable Valentine's Day dinner. She helped coach him through the breakup, and in turn shared a lot about herself and her experience with Nigel. They had gone for coffee twice while Colt was still in Pink Shell Shores, before he returned to Manhattan for work in the third week of February. Of course, Bell knew that he needed time to heal. She hardly expected him to drop everything, start a new relationship with her, and move to Pink Shell Shores.

Well, perhaps a *small* part of her did.

"Thank you for everything, Bell," Colt had said before leaving. "I won't forget this."

Still, Bell hummed through her days. Already, two of the weddings she had planned had been featured in bridal magazines. Today, she opened up a gift from Clayton and Mallory, a couple whose wedding she had recently planned.

"We couldn't have done it without you," the card wrote. "You kept us calm, sane, and happy throughout the whole process. We can't thank you enough!!!" it said.

Bell smiled and placed the card on her desk. A knock came from her door.

"Come in!" Bell called. In walked Penny, looking radiant. "You're right on time!" Bell beamed. Within the past two months, Bell had become better friends with Penny and Chantal. Now, Bell had finally agreed to have her palm read by Penny. In her limited time, her lunch break at the Wisteria Estate seemed to be all she could manage.

"It looks amazing in here!" Penny gushed. Bell flushed. She had to admit, her office looked fantastic. She had brought accents of fuchsia in the curtains and gone to a million junk shops to find the perfect gold accents—from the throw pillows, the vases. Even her new desk had a coat of gold paint. She breathed a sigh of relief. It *did* look amazing.

"Alright, whenever you're ready," Penny began, taking a seat across from Bell. "We can begin your reading."

Bell held out her palm. She had never had her fortune told before and felt surprisingly nervous. "What do you see?" she asked Penny.

Penny's eyes sprang to life. "It's funny. I see someone arriving in your life. Unexpectedly. Someone who you perhaps at one point had feelings for."

The color drained from Bell's face. "Oh, is that so?" she asked.

Penny nodded enthusiastically. "That's not all. He'll be arriving..." she checked her watch. "Now."

Bell nearly fell off her chair as Colt walked into her office, a sly smile overcoming him.

"She's good, huh?" Colt said, motioning to Penny. Penny laughed.

Bell looked from Colt to Penny. "So, this was planned?"

Penny winked in Colt's direction. "You're on. Bell," Penny said, turning to Bell. "I still have to do your reading one of these days."

Colt stood in front of Bell. It had been just less than two months since she had last seen him. He seemed to be studying her face.

"What are you doing here?" she breathed.

Colt smiled. "My sister and her family still live here. Remember?"

Bell did remember, as she nodded. "Right, right."

Colt was quick to recover. "But I wanted to see you too."

She felt her cheeks turning pink. "Really?"

"I've had some time to think about things since I've been gone," Colt said, taking a seat across from her. "I have something I wanted to tell you."

Bell's eyebrows shot up. "What's that?"

"I'm moving to Pink Shell Shores," Colt declared. "I'm going to run my business from here. And I don't know if it will be weird or not, given that we'll be neighbors, but I wanted to officially ask you out. Like, on a date," he clarified.

Bell could have screamed, she was that ecstatic. Instead, putting her nerves aside, she smiled. "No," she began, seeing Colt's face fall. "I mean, no, I don't think that's weird at all!" she quickly clarified.

Colt smiled. "Right. So, are you free after work?"

Bell pulled a face. "I have to head home and take Georgia for a walk first."

"I love spending time with Georgia," Colt said. "Mind if I join?"

Bell grinned. "I don't mind one bit."

The End

Acknowledgements

I would like to thank my wonderful husband, Ryan, for your continued support and love. You are my eternal inspiration. I want to thank my family—you guys give me the confidence to feel like I can do anything. Finally, I want to extend a huge thank you to you, dear reader. I wouldn't be able to continue doing what I love without your support. *If you enjoyed reading this book, a review would mean the world to me.* Thank you.

About the Author

KAYA QUINSEY HOLT IS the author of F*ate at the Wisteria Estate (The Pink Shell Shores Series Volume 1)*, as well as *The Marseille Millionaire, Paris Mends Broken Hearts, Valentine in Venice,* and *A Coastal Christmas.* She lives in Toronto with her husband and their puppy.

www.kayaquinsey.com
www.goodreads.com/kayaquinsey
Twitter: @KayaQuinseyHolt
Instagram: @KayaQuinseyHolt

Turn the page for an exciting peak into Kaya's upcoming book, **The Belles of Positano.** Available March 28, 2020.

Sneak Peak: The Belles of Positano

Clara Belle's older sister, Lorena Belle, swished around in her wedding gown. Lorena gave their mother and Clara a twirl. The late afternoon sunlight dappled through the open windows and Clara took another swig of her San Pellegrino.

"It's just perfect," Lorena breathed, as she beamed at her reflection in the gold gilded mirror.

Their mother's eyes widened. "It's... well... beautiful," she said, darting a nervous glance in Clara's direction. "But... but why is it *blue*?"

It was the elephant in the room, which none of them had dared to mention since the dress had arrived by courier late the night before. Clara had desperately been hoping that it was just the moonlight, casting an eerie blue glow against the tulle. But nope. It was blue. *Blue.* Not a subtle shade of blue either. There was no doubt about it.

To Clara's complete surprise, Lorena seems unfazed as she twirled for herself in front of the mirror. Sure, Clara knew that Lorena was fairly relaxed. Much unlike herself. They were extremes at the opposites ends of that spectrum; one of the many ways in which the sisters were different. But, Clara hadn't thought it possible to be that relaxed with the wedding only one week away. Lorena shrugged, maintaining her air of unfazed contentment. Nothing was going to ruin her wedding, Clara realized. Not even a blue dress.

"It's not *dark* blue," Lorena said brightly, as if that made it seem normal. "It's more of a light turquoise. Besides, it matches the water!" The three of them turned toward the open floor-to-ceiling window, which overlooked the Tyrrhenian Sea. Lorena was right. Now that Clara looked at the dress more closely, there was some intricate beadwork that seemed to mimic the sun shimmering on the water.

"I should have known better than to let you order a dress online," their mother, Dahlia Belle fretted, as if not having heard a word her older daughter had said. "And we have everyone coming from West Palm Beach," she continued, clutching her pearls. "We have *got* to find you another dress. Clara, what's open?" There was an urgent expression on her mother's taught face.

Now it was Clara's turn to shrug. "Mama, it's Sunday," she replied with a sigh. "*Nothing* here is open on a Sunday."

It was true. They had all landed in Positano—the sunny, cliff-side Italian village—only a few days earlier. Even back in Florida, Clara couldn't begin to imagine where one would pick up a last minute wedding gown. Now that they were in Italy, it seemed even more unfathomable.

Her mother exhaled sharply. Clara could practically see her mother's mind working a mile a minute, trying to figure out a solution to what only *she* considered a problem. If there was one thing that Dahlia Belle was determined to do, it was to make sure that her only two daughters had the weddings that they (or *she*) had always dreamed of.

Of course, for Dahlia Belle, that meant a country club wedding near their home in West Palm Beach. But, for Lorena, a dream wedding meant getting married in Positano with a view of the Mediterranean Sea. Now that Clara was finally there, she could see why. Originally a small fishing village set along cliffs of the Western coast of Italy, Positano radiated every bit of *la dolce vita* that Clara had dreamed Italy would be. And then some.

Along jagged seaside hills were some of the most striking pastel houses, all nestled up against one another. The tomatoes in Clara's caprese salad the day before had tasted more tomato-y any tomato she had ever had. The light seemed more golden, the food more delicious, the atmosphere more romantic. The gold and white church, the Santa Maria Assunta, towered over the rest of the buildings in Positano. There were strict building codes here. No mega-hotel chains. No seafront condominiums. Life here seemed slow like honey. Clara was enjoying every moment of it.

Clara was the maid of honor, and the only bridesmaid, at her sister's wedding. Lorena was destined to marry Lyle Richardson, her high school sweetheart and partner in...*whatever* it was they were doing.

Seven years earlier, Lorena and Lyle had decided to backpack through Europe during the summer between high school and college. But Dahlia Belle had another plan for her eldest daughter. Lorena was supposed to go to Duke. Lorena didn't seem to see things that way, even though she had already been accepted and the checks had been written. Lorena and Lyle were only supposed to have travelled through Europe for one-month before beginning college.

As the summer came to an end back in West Palm Beach, Clara and her parents had gotten a postcard from Lorena, who at the time had been in Italy. Lorena wrote to say that she wasn't coming back to North America for at least a few months. Clara recalled her poor mother's panic, calling and threatening Lorena to come get her from Italy herself and drag her back home, if that's what it took. All the while, Lorena would send Clara secret text messages, telling her that she just *had* to come visit. That life in Italy was surreal. That she had never done anything so exciting.

Clara had wanted to, more than anything, but she had only been in the tenth grade at the time. Her pocket money could barely get her a bus ticket to New York City, let alone a flight to Italy. It was all quite dramatic. Their mother had threatened to cut Lorena off. But Lyle's trust fund had already come into effect, so Lorena no longer needed their parents or their money. Clara remembered it was the first time she had ever seen her mother look truly sad. Her father, of course, had hauled himself up in his office, working even longer hours than usual.

Clara was two years younger than Lorena. After Lorena decided that college wasn't for her, and she instead began teaching English across the sea, her mother sank all of her ambition onto Clara. Vanderbilt was where her mother now had her pegged at attending. It was where Clara had just graduated from with a degree in psychology with absolutely no idea about her next steps.

Clara took a deep breath, ignoring her mother and instead focusing on the view. It was pretty magnificent. Their hotel, *Il Grande Sirena*, doubled both as their accommodation and as the venue for the wedding. Perched halfway up the cliff, the hotel had magnificent views that overlooked the sea and had the best patio for watching sunsets. Pastel-colored houses dotted the steep hill beneath them, with a perfect and unmarred view of the beach. Clara had to hand it to her sister—Lorena had nailed it with her choice of wedding destination.

Their hotel room, where Lorena continued to twirl and admire herself, had a small adjacent terrace. Opening up the French-style doors, Clara felt herself relax as she breathed in that unmistakable Positano air—fresh from the sea with a pungent note of diesel fumes from the cars that travelled down the steep winding roads. Clara grabbed her phone to take a picture for her Instagram account, which was already flooded with pictures of wishy-washy walkways, *very* full glasses of prosecco, and pictures of her at the beach. She hadn't done all of those sit-ups in the months leading up to this event for nothing.

"Darling," Dahlia Belle trilled. "You don't happen to have a *date* for the wedding, do you?" Although her voice sounded innocent, Clara knew the sub-text. Find a man. Or I'll find one for you. Dahlia Belle had done it at weddings before; no doubt, she would do it again.

Clara took a deep breath, doing her best to keep her tone even. "No, mom. We're in Italy. We're in *Positano*. Unless he came in my luggage, there are no men here for me."

Visit Kaya Quinsey Holt's website at

www.kayaquinsey.com

Printed in Great Britain
by Amazon

29516269R00059